THE MAKING OF THE WORLD

"In the beginning, Maha of the Holy Fire was alone in the world that she had made. Then she brought forth four children: Voiha the Wise, Great Rehera, Nité the Spoiler, and Karathek her son.

"Since the world's beginning, Voiha has dreamed, and her voice has not spoken aloud. But Karathek, who loved her, went into her dreams, and with his hands fashioned what Voiha dreamed—first the stars, then the Immortals, and then the lesser creatures: birds and beasts and all that grows, and mortal women. All these he made, but they had no life. Then Rehera looked upon them, and all that was fair she breathed upon, and they began to live

"Then Karathek fashioned for Voiha a couch of silver and for himself a chair of copper, and he set them in heaven. And there they shine, so that night is made holy as day and the dreams of Voiha watch over the dreams of mortals. But Rehera remained in the world, and she watches over it; and so it shall be until Voiha wakes and speaks aloud again."

WHEN VOIHA WAKES
A masterpiece of fantasy by JOY CHANT

Author of *The High Kings, Red Moon and Black Mountain* and *The Grey Mane of Morning*

Other Bantam Books by Joy Chant
Ask your bookseller for the titles you have missed

THE GREY MANE OF MORNING
RED MOON AND BLACK MOUNTAIN

WHEN VOIHA WAKES

JOY CHANT

BANTAM BOOKS
TORONTO · NEW YORK · LONDON · SYDNEY

WHEN VOIHA WAKES
A Bantam Book / November 1983

ISBN 0-553-23647-4

Published simultaneously in the United States and Canada

Bantam Books are published by Bantam Books, Inc. Its trade-
mark, consisting of the words "Bantam Books" and the por-
trayal of a rooster, is Registered in U.S. Patent and Trademark
Office and in other countries. Marca Registrada. Bantam
Books, Inc., 666 Fifth Avenue, New York, New York 10103.

PRINTED IN THE UNITED STATES OF AMERICA

O   0 9 8 7 6 5 4 3 2 1

for
JACK
who heard it through
and saw me through

The setting of this story is southwestern Vandarei; the time, about that of the arrival of the Harani in Kedrinh.

WHEN VOIHA WAKES

I

Rahiké had parted from the caravan at noon, and now the sun was shining in her face, so that she had to tip her sunhat forward to shade her eyes. It was not far now to the hillcrest where the road turned down into Naramethé, and from the border to the City was no great journey. She should be home before evening. There would be time to see the Mistress briefly, time to complete the day's business, without delaying the moment when she could see Burdal again. At the thought of her child her strides lengthened. Baby, baby . . . if only you had been younger, I could have taken you with me. Many women in the caravan had carried infants, but Burdal was almost four, a difficult age for such a journey, so Rahiké had left her with her own mother.

Beside her the cart bounced and rattled. The brown donkey and the gray leaned their heads together as if commenting on the steepness of the road. Rahiké pushed a stone aside from a wheel with her staff and steadied some of the bundles. "Almost home, little sisters," she said. Their small hooves moved lightly through the grass and stones, quick and neat. In comparison her tread seemed slow, and she leaned on her staff as she walked; but her strides pushed the miles steadily behind her, as they had done for weeks, through half of Halilak, south to the great city and back again.

1

Rahiké was a handsome woman, slender and upright, of middle height, though her bearing made her seem taller. She moved with vigor and grace; her body and limbs were firm and smooth, her face was the true Halilaki oval with strong fine features, and her shapely hands were almost unblemished, not calloused and scarred with field work. She wore her curling black hair rather long for a woman, halfway down her back; but her tawny-brown eyes belied this girlishness, for they were reserved, clear rather than bright. Plenty of men would have been glad to catch her eye, but for years she had taken little interest in them. Working with the Mistress took most of her time, and the rest belonged to Burdal. At twenty-eight she had lost none of the energy of youth, but it was controlled, and the exuberance of earlier years had become an alert calm.

She was clothed like most Halilaki women, in long loose trousers. A small bodice supported her breasts, but her smock lay in the cart, for though summer had not yet come the day was hot. It had made half the pleasure of the journey north, walking up into the warmth. The breeze fanned her body pleasantly; she rested her staff across her shoulders and leaned her wrists against it. When the donkeys paused at a stream she pulled off her sunhat and headcloth, shaking her hair to let the cool air run through it. It was very dirty. She had not washed it since leaving Halkal-Mari, only ducked it sometimes swimming. As soon as she reached her mother's house she would bathe; it would be good to feel clogged with dirt no longer.

Since leaving the road she had been walking through empty country, for there was space to spare in Halilak in those days, and the people lived in the rich valleys, leaving the poorer lands uncultivated. About her now were only birds, and along the hillside a few deer, but looking back the way she had come she could see in the distance, beyond the road, the fields and orchards of Karserik. Her own border was close; soon she could see the head of the pass, and the pillars set up either side of the road, the name "Naramethé" carved on each. Her pace quickened: for a moment her eyes blurred, and she cleared her throat in surprise. But when she came to the crest, she had to stop. She was not prepared for the emotion that seized her. Before her feet the road ran down into Naramethé, she was in her own land, her feet on its soil: she was acutely aware of that contact with the earth, as if the aching gladness that filled her were drawn up through her soles. Briefly, confusion gripped her; she swallowed, frowned, and laughed; then busied herself about the cart, putting the drag on the wheels. There was someone coming up the narrow path, and it was hard to pass in any place but that, so she sat down on a rock to wait, looking into the dale.

To north and south the broad valley lay, her realm, her home. When she had left it winter had not long ended, but now all was green and blossoming. Cornfields and orchards lay spread below her, woodlands, vine slopes, and the precious spice gardens, and through it all wound bright Nára and her streams. In the south were the wide expanses of the public lands where most of the wheat was grown, but in the north the farms were smaller and the houses more numerous. The hillsides above the cultivated lands were crowded with shrines to the many goddesses of Halilak; only the very greatest, wise Voiha and great Rehera and holy Maha herself, had temples in the valley. Higher than the shrines, higher even than the summer pastures, were the mines that gave Naramethé half her trade wealth. Far beyond them, immense and vague, were the mountains. Rahiké's people had no neighbors over their western border. On other sides lay Ruthathé, Sikas, Hirmethé, Karserik, and others Rahiké had not seen, that were only names to her. Farther still were countries known only by rumor, and in the remote north, if report were true, the scandalous places where women kept men in their houses: and beyond that, the darkness. Legend spoke of a wilderness and desert at the world's edge, but of no more. In those days in Halilak they had never heard of lands where men ruled, or of nations who made war.

The shadowy north could not hold Rahiké's eyes from her bright valley.

It was not a large country, though prosperous, being one of the Spice Lands as well as having mines. To none of its children was it dearer than to Rahiké, who gazed with cherishing love on the land she would one day govern. Almost at its heart, not very far from where she was, Nára ran to her meeting with a smaller river, and there stood the City and the Market and the Town. The smallest of these was the most important; most of the women of Naramethé lived on their farms, and the size of their City had always been a joke among them. Now that Rahiké had seen the magnificence of Halkal-Mari it did make her smile, but very gently. Below it in the angle of the rivers stood the Market, and across Nára was the Men's Town, much larger than the City and very different, with its wall and its long lodges. Smoke was hanging thickly over their thatched roofs, telling her she had not come home on a holiday. The Halilaki of that time loved play as they do now, and holidays were many: every ninth day, the full and the new of either moon, the feasts of the greater goddesses and of the solitary god, and for the Town the days of their craft-heroes. But Rahiké scarcely glanced at the Town: it was at her City she gazed. She could distinguish the colored tiles of the larger buildings, the Temple of the Holy Fire, the Children's Court, the Meeting House, the Law Court, the house of the Mistress, and the schools. Her own house north of the City she could not see, it was too far; but she could just pick out her mother's farm. There, if her eyes could have found them, her family were working in the fields; and Burdal was with them. At that thought the immensity of her love gathered to a point and pierced her. She stood up with a groan of impatience, and stared down the road.

The other traveler was near the crest. Rahiké recognized her, an official from Karserik whom she had met several times, and called out a greeting; the other waved, but said nothing until she stopped by her, when she gasped and wiped her face. "This road is all very well for people as slim as you; I'm not built for it," she said.

"You should have taken a rest."

"Couldn't. Saw you waiting." She fanned herself with her hat, and said, "I'll be the first to ask: What's the great city like?"

"Oh—all you've ever heard and more." She eyed the donkeys' panniers; they were so light, they could only contain one thing, and she grinned. "Incense-gum?"

"What else? We heard you were putting the price up, so our priestesses got onto the Old Lady, and off I had to go. And only just in time, I see."

"Yes indeed." She patted one of the boxes in her cart. "It's written down in Halkal-Mari, and I've got the copies here."

"What's it to be, then?" Rahiké told her and she whistled. "Nice for you, having all there is of something like that."

"It isn't as high as we wanted; won't bring our revenue near what it was before the blight. And it's only for five years. We would have to apply again then; but we should have replaced our losses in that time—as they told me!"

"Oh, well, if Halkal-Mari accepts it I suppose it's fair." She put her hat on again and shortened the donkey's lead-rope. "Well, I'm sure you've got someone waiting for you—"

"Yes. My little girl. And you've a long way to go yet. Never mind, it's mostly downhill now. Call on me next time you come; good-bye, Nadéha."

When she came to the City the yellows and ochres in the paint were standing out from the other colors, blazing back the sun's richness. There was no wall, no gate, but halfway up from the bridge grew a solitary tree that was a favorite loitering place. There Rahiké gathered an escort of young girls, who were still darting and chattering about her when she came to the Mistress's porch. "What was Halkal-Mari like?—How far did you walk every day?—Can I take the donkeys?—Is it cold there?—Did you see the Queen?—Were your shoes comfortable? My uncle made your shoes.—Can I take the donkeys?"

"No one may touch the donkeys unless Nehsa says they may. But you can go and tell her I am back. Who else will go errands for me?" They jumped about eagerly and ran off as she directed them. Zeriha the doctor had needed no fetching; she was already hurrying across the court; nothing Rahiké had brought from the south was more precious than her box of medicines. Some of the girls Rahiké sent with bundles to her own house. Then she pulled on her smock, retied her headcloth and cast her hat into the cart, sorted a number of boxes from the luggage and allowed two of the quietest girls to carry them for her, and asked the remainder to guard the cart. They ranged themselves grimly about it; she grinned, picked up her last bundle, and went in.

Less than an hour later she was on the path to her mother's farm. The way lay by the garden kept by her friend Mekiné, and after hesitating briefly she turned in at the gate. Mekiné was working among the incense bushes, covering them against the risk of a late frost; she called a greeting and said, "I'll be done in a moment." Her baby was splashing happily in the water trenches, and her little boy stood near. Seeing Rahiké he broke into smiles and came trotting toward her, his hands held up. "Look what I did!" he cried.

She crouched down and took what he offered her, while he stood rubbing his feet together, gazing soberly from her face to his handiwork. It was grubby and warped, but recognizably a strip of weaving. Rahiké turned admiring eyes on him.

"Did you do this, Naniel?"

His mother, coming out from the bushes, stood watching

with a smile. The child nodded seriously. "I did it." he said. "I did *weave* it." He spoke the craft word with emphasis, alight with pride. Rahiké exclaimed in wonder, and gave the piece back to him. As she rose she pressed his hands in hers, saying with approving warmth, "Clever hands!"

Naniel beamed widely. "Uncle Tirek showed me how. Uncle Tirek is a Master!"

"Well, and so will you be, won't you?"

"Yes: when I am big."

"Will you be a weaver like Uncle Tirek?"

But he was lost for an answer to that, only squirmed his shoulders and laughed. His mother called, "Say, 'Don't be silly, Madam Rahiké, I'm only four!'" The child looked up at the smiling woman and repeated, "I'm only four." Rahiké stroked his hair; "Only four, and already you can weave!"

When Naniel had run into the house with his treasure Rahiké said, "How like Tirek he is growing; I never noticed before." Mekiné flushed slightly; the share men had in the making of children was knowledge kept so secret by the women that they rarely spoke of it even among themselves. Mekiné was deferential to such conventions, and although twenty years of friendship had accustomed her to Rahiké's greater freedom, it had not hardened her against embarrassment. "Yes; but it is his gestures, I think, more than his face."

Her friend looked at her with a faint smile. "It has been a long time."

"More than five years," said Mekiné calmly, free of embarrassment just when most women would have felt it. "You took Rithakel soon after."

Rahiké laughed. "So I did." She understood Mekiné's fidelity no more than others, but was too fond of her to mock it. Now she made a pounce toward the grubby toddler at her friend's heels. "Well, little lady, remember me? You've got steadier legs than when I left. Eeeh, look at you, you muddy little object—oh, you're so muddy, I never saw such mud; you little ditch-digger, what's to be done with you? Put her under the pump, the little urchin!"

The child ran round her mother's legs, shrieking with laughter, and Mekiné caught her up, smiling. "She's been helping me with the bushes, haven't you? But bath for you now, Miss! Are you in a hurry, Rahiké? Shall I make you a drink?"

Rahiké shook her head. "No, I must go—Burdal—I mustn't stay. I'll come and tell you all about it soon. I really came with a message, odd as it sounds. When you see your brother, tell him to come to my house some evening."

Mekiné stared at her: and in her face Rahiké saw not only amazement but some concern she had to allay. "It's only that he asked me to buy something for him—on his behalf, that is—in the south. Tell him I have it, whenever he cares to fetch it."

"Mairilek asked you to—! O, Holy Fire, it *would* be Mairilek! He must be forgetting who you are now. I ask pardon for him, Raha; he never *means* any harm. He's a good boy, but such a fool."

"Oh, there was no harm. Who could be offended with him?" Mekiné's face grew suspicious again, and Rahiké laughed aloud. "What's the matter with you, Meké? You're growling like a nursery dog! Do you think I'm going to attack your little brother? I was thinking of his manners, that's all; not his face." She remembered him best as a little boy in awe of his big sister's friend; he had been charming then, too.

Mekiné smiled, shamefaced. "Yes, of course. You can't let such things—not that you would—I suppose I worry too much about Mairilek. But it isn't always good fortune for boys as foolish as he is to have looks like his."

Rahiké picked up her bundle and they walked together to the gate. "Is he such a fool? He didn't talk like one." She had barely exchanged a dozen words with him since he went to the Town, until their last meeting. What the

sweet-tempered child might have become she could not
guess.

"Maybe not; but he acts like one."

"And so his big sister thinks she ought to protect him
from wicked women. What harm could they do him?"

"Make him unhappy," said Mekiné flatly. Rahiké looked
at her, and was suddenly torn between indignation and
amusement.

"Great Rehera, did you think—is that why you glared
at me?" A child's shining face peered round a door in her
memory, and made the thought even more outrageous.
Mekiné looked confused, and mumbled some disclaimer.
"Was I sending for him, then? And through his sister!
There are privileges for being the Young Mistress, but that
is not one of them!"

She was still grinning at her friend's discomfiture as
she went on toward her mother's farm. The truth was,
she thought, that natural partiality made Mekiné overrate
her brother's beauty and exaggerate its effects. She herself
could not recall his face clearly, though it had won him
fame. Mekiné and her mother, Tiridal, had a round-faced
comeliness; she could imagine that in a boy this might
become lush enough for beauty. Since his apprenticeship
she had seen him too rarely for his present appearance to
displace the child from her mind. And at their last meeting,
although he had amazed her, it had not been by his face.

She had set out for Halkal-Mari on a morning when
spring seemed to be returning to winter. Her road crossed
a river twice, and by the second bridge Mairilek had been
waiting. He must have walked miles from the Town, by
night, in the rain, to accost her there. His clothes were
heavy with water, he was muddy, his hair drenched about
his pinched face; he was hunched against the cold. Only
when he gave his name did she know him for her friend's
brother, the family beauty. Rahiké had still been raw from
her parting with Burdal, and was at first inclined to be
brusque with Mairilek's temerity, in no humor to wait in

the rain to talk to a boy. But his courtesy compelled hers, and she was arrested by such boldness in one reputed to be so shy, so she had listened to him. He had given her, as he said, all the money he possessed, and had asked humbly if, while she was in Halkal-Mari, she would see if it was enough to buy a musical instrument.

At that she had hooked up the reins and turned to stare down at him indeed. "A musical instrument!"

He had nodded, his face tensing painfully. She said brusquely, "What, a tambour, a pipe, a sistrum?"

"No, no. There are other kinds, more complicated, more—like—"

"Well, I know that! I have seen musicians, you know." Though in fact she had seen none for ten years, and not heeded them much then. He winced with embarrassment, and she relented a little. "Though what you want with such a thing, I can't think. Well, and you think they make them in Halkal-Mari?"

"Oh surely! If not there, then where? If—if you will buy me anything the money will get—if it will get one at all. I beg you, Madam Rahiké!"

His fervor impressed her; she could not refuse. She had taken the purse he held up, and been surprised at its weight. "Well, there should be enough here, by the feel of it! But I still don't see why you want one."

His face had tensed a little more, and he dropped his eyes. "Ever since the musicians came—they seemed marvelous things, so strange—I always wanted to, to see one—to have one—"

"Oh, it's no affair of mine. I'm not your Master." However strange, it clearly mattered a great deal to him. "But you have not told me what sort you want. Have they names?"

"I don't know." For an instant there had been agony in his eyes. "I don't know," he cried apologetically, his voice grown strong with distress. "One with strings?—please, with strings. I don't know!"

*　　*　　*

Her mother was not home when she reached the farm; no one was in the house but her great-aunt, and when Rahiké began politely to talk to her, she laughed and waved her away. So she hurried thankfully out of the back of the house, across the courtyard, onto the path that led down to the fields, and she had got no further than the first bend when she saw them. They shouted her name and waved, but Rahiké gave one call and ran, for out of their midst burst a small figure who scampered up the path toward her with high squeals of joy, and she ran to snatch her daughter up into her arms. Rahiké laughed and wept, but Burdal gave one sob and was silent as she wound arms and legs about her mother, gripping her hair and pushing her face against her, while Rahiké kissed her and held her and vowed uselessly that never, never again, not even when she was Mistress, never would she be parted from her child even for a night.

Later, greetings over and gifts distributed, while Burdal sat on the floor playing with her gift from the far city and Rahiké, clean and cool now with damp hair about her shoulders, helped her mother spread the meal, she asked, "Was she good?"

"Of course she was. She quarreled over a toy sometimes, but she was very good for a child who is not used to sharing anything. You should have another, Rahiké." She only laughed. "We had a few tears the first nights, of course, but not too bad."

"And Heffa stayed with me," said Burdal, joining in unexpectedly. "Heffa slept by my bed every night, and I wasn't scared. But tonight I'll sleep in my own bed, won't I, in my own house?"

"Yes you will; and I will be sleeping in my bed in the front room. Was Heffa good?"

"Quite good. And Aunt Mirrik took me every day to see the other dogs, and sometimes we went twice, and sometimes Aunt Siké came or Sinak and we played games with them." She spoke composedly, but suddenly she left her toy and went to her mother, leaning against her leg and holding hard to it. "Don't go away again," came her muffled whisper. "I don't like you to."

Sunset had faded to dusk when they went down to their home, and their long shadows were very dim, though the thatch of the Men's Town on the opposite hillside still shone. Burdal walked sleepily, one hand holding her mother's, the other gripped in the coat of her dog, Heffa, one of the huge shaggy breed of nursery dogs that the women of Halilak kept to guard their children. Rahiké's was a good house, a handsome house, befitting the Young Mistress: it stood alone, a little north of the City and nearer to the river, close by a small wood. It was built against a steep slope, so that the porch was high from the ground with a place beneath it where the dogs lay and space under the long front room for a store. Most households had a number of dogs; Rahiké had five besides Heffa—four guard dogs and one smaller, the porch dog. Now as they approached all these began to run about at the end of their long chains, barking and yelping. Burdal came wide awake for a moment, and looked at her mother laughing.

Rahiké knew her sisters would have kept the house clean for her, but she had expected to find it dark and chill on her return. But there was a faint glow through the orange blinds, a thread of smoke from the chimney, and someone had kindled the hanging lamp that lit the porch. The welcome warmed her. She had not lived in the house long, it was not yet a year since it had been built for her, but she loved it dearly. Later, when Burdal was asleep, she took a lamp and wandered slowly through it all, the back room, the kitchen, the wash-houses, touching and greeting; strolling round the courtyard to see how her plants grew, and the vine, and the blossoming tree; fondling the two dogs who lived there. Indoors again she moved about the long room that ran along the front of the house, repossessing it; the polished wooden floor bright with rugs, the raised walled hearth with its decorated

canopy and the low platform beside it where her bed was
spread, the carved chest and shelves in the opposite alcove,
the bench under the window and her chair. The little fire
dancing on the hearth was enough to make the colors of the
room, the oranges, yellows, reds, beloved of Rahiké's people,
glow brighter. Everything in the house, whether for use or
ornament, was a miracle of craftsmanship. But Rahiké took
that for granted. It was not the beauty of it she was
savoring, but the delight of being in her own home again.

After a while she poured herself a cup of thinned
wine and filled her pipe, and went to sit on the porch.
There were benches there, but she preferred the steps.
Being high from the ground her porch was railed, with a
short railed staircase. All, the stair rails, the balustrade,
the roofposts, were carved and painted. Rahiké sat quiet,
sipping the drink, savoring the fragrant smoke. It was
quite dark now; in the east before her both the moons
were rising together, and the sky was speckled with glinting
stars. Across the shallow valley the windows in the Lodges
shone brightly, but Rahiké scarcely noticed them. All the
beautiful things about her, from the glories of her house to
the clothes she wore and the cup and pipe in her hand,
had been made by men from that town: and in all the
world there were not nor have there been since any
craftsmen to equal the craftsmen of old Halilak. But
Rahiké and her people knew nothing of the rest of the
world, and she would have been surprised only if beauty
had failed to come out of the Lodges. The Men's Town was
in her gaze, but not in her mind. Slowly the evening grew
cool, and became night. She had finished her cup and her
pipe, so she fetched the little dog who lay all night on the
porch, and went in to bed.

"In the beginning," said the Halilaki, "Maha of the
Holy Fire was in the world that she had made. She was
alone in the world. Then she brought forth four children,

but they did not wake at once. She bore Voiha, and Rehera, and Nité, and Karathek her son. Then while they slept she rose into the heavens to look without ceasing on all that she had made; for when heaven and earth were new, there was not any night.

"Then she bade her children wake, and they rose, and walked in the world. Voiha was the greatest of them, though Rehera was filled with the Fire of Maha. Karathek had neither knowledge nor understanding, but he was full of love and delight, happy in the light of Maha. But Nité envied her sisters. She walked less and less with them, and at last not at all. In her solitude she grew to hate them, and to hate even the Fire of Maha. She sought a place where Maha could not look upon her, but there was no such place; Maha gazed on all that she had made. Then Nité resolved to make a place where Maha could not come, and with great labor she bent the world that was still new and changeable, so that half of it lay in darkness, and the Fire of Maha could not warm it.

"The other children of Maha, even Voiha the Wise, had thought no evil of Nité, for there had not been such a thing in the world until then. But when they saw what she had done, they were dismayed and wrathful. Voiha sought her sister in the darkness, and found her, and there they strove together. But even in the darkness Voiha's spirit was the stronger, and she overcame the will of Nité, and brought her before the face of Maha once more. Then in the light of the Holy Fire Nité saw herself, and her heart fell, and she shriveled and wailed and fled: and her part in the rule of the world was taken from her. Then Maha made the world to turn before her so that she saw all parts of it once more; for the night could not be unmade.

"But the struggle with Nité had been hard, and Voiha was weary. She lay down and slept, and she did not wake: and since the world's beginning Voiha the Wise has not spoken aloud. Yet in her sleep she dreamed. Then Karathek, who loved her, went into her dreams, and with his hands he fashioned what Voiha dreamed. First of her dreams he made the stars, to catch the Fire of Maha and burn in the darkness Nité had made. Then she dreamed other things, and they came from Karathek's hands; the Immortals first, and then the lesser creatures: beasts and birds and all that grows, and mortal women. All these he made, but they had no life. Then Rehera took them and looked upon them, and some she set aside; for not all that Voiha dreamed was good. At times her sleep was troubled with thoughts of Nité, but whatever Karathek found there he brought into being, both good and bad, for he could not distinguish between them. Yet most was fair, and these Rehera breathed upon, and they began to live.

"But Nité came in secret, and stole what Rehera set aside. She could not give them life unless she took that life from some creature to whom Rehera had given it; and this she sought to do, and still seeks to do. Sometimes Nité steals a life before Rehera takes it back to herself, and then a creature of Voiha's bad dreams can live. And she is Nité the Spoiler, and all evil and sorrow are from her. It is she puts the worm in the fruit, the venom in the snake, and the pain in childbed.

"Then the world lived and grew and changed, and Rehera delighted in it. But Voiha still slept. Then Karathek made the last of his great works, and these Voiha had not dreamed. He fashioned for her a couch of silver, and for himself a chair of copper, and he set them in heaven. Then he laid Voiha on her couch, and sat himself in his chair to wait by her. And there they shine, so that night is made holy as day and the dreams of Voiha watch over the dreams of mortals. But Rehera remained in the world, and she watches over it; and so it shall be until Voiha wakes and speaks aloud again."

So went the tale of the beginning of things that they told long ago in Halilak. Such was the belief of Rahiké and her people; and in her time they still divided the world as in the story. Wisdom and authority and the power to give life belonged to the daughters of Maha, and her son was a maker. So it was in Halilak. The women worshipped Rehera above others, and had motherhood and government and care for all the earth gave for their part in life; while the men served Karathek the Hundred-Handed, and for them there was the exercise of craftmanship and the companionship of other men. Property passed from mothers to daughters; learning was shared only among the women, and all the work that needed wisdom belonged to them. It was natural, they reasoned, that it should be so: for women had children, and their first care was for them, so their minds were of necessity upon the future. Responsibility and foresight were forced upon women, but for men it was not so. They cared most for their own deeds and the esteem of other men; their concern was with the present, and it was not their nature to think ahead. It was their glory to enrich and beautify the world, but not to guide it.

And men agreed to this; but often they said among themselves; it was Karathek who heard the dreams of the Dreamer; and for all their wisdom women made nothing new, with their hands or with their minds.

By the evening of the fourth day after her return Rahiké began to feel the wound of her absence healing. She had taken up her work again, and caught up with all the concerns of her family, and she had spent a whole evening in playing with Burdal. The child was growing calm again, the first raptures of reunion over. Soon, thought her mother, she would begin to misbehave, and then everything would be normal.

That evening she had no visitors. Burdal was sitting on the floor in her own room, singing tunelessly, moving her dolls about, breaking off her song to tell Heffa what was happening to them. Rahiké stood by the window, listening and smiling. She was hardly heeding anything she saw, her mind on the child's chatter, but after a while her eye was caught by a distant figure, a boy or a young man, running on the hills. Her first thought was that they were holding one of their Games, and she looked for the others, but he was alone. Besides, rumor of a Games usually got about; young women and girls liked to go and watch. When she looked again a little later she saw him again. He was coming toward the river and the road to the City. There were always men on the roads in the evening, coming over Nára to visit lovers or kin, though mostly earlier than this. Perhaps that was why he was running. A belt of trees hid him briefly, and she watched for him to reappear where below her house a bend in the river brought the hills near. Then he broke from the trees into her plain view: and she gasped aloud, and forgot to listen to Burdal.

It had been long since Rahiké had looked on men to admire them. A boy's pretty face might catch her eye, but she had forgotten their bodies, forgotten the hard agile strength that was their glory. Now the beauty of men smote her as if for the first time.

He was young, clad only in a blue kilt, and he ran easily, as if for delight as much as haste. His skin was lightly tanned, so that his broad shoulders, his wide flat chest and deep sides, shone like oiled wood. He kept his back upright, his head high, and at every bound his long black hair rose away from his face and bounced back onto his shoulders. Straight and swift he came, springing down the hillside light as a young hart. So might Hiramarrek himself appear, fairest of the sons of women, he who woke desire even in Nehaté of the Frosts, and now flees her forever around the earth, fearing to die in her cold embrace.

He did not go down to the bridge but crossed Nára by the stepping-stones, changing his stride but not checking his speed, spreading his arms for each leap. Rahiké found that she was leaning out of the window to watch him, and recollecting herself she drew back and turned away, ashamed to do so longer. He thought himself unobserved, running with unselfconscious grace; it seemed unkind to stare at him in secret. Still, the vision would not leave her mind. Certainly she had ignored the Town too long, forgotten too much. A few moments later she glanced out of her window again. He was standing among the trees near her house smoothing his hair. He was coming to see her.

Astonished, she caught up her headcloth and tied it about her hair, then went out onto the porch. He was running again. She could see his face now; a pure oval, with features perfectly molded. For an instant Rahiké's blood seemed to run backwards; then she returned to the ordinary world, her common sense restored. She laughed, moving to the rail. She knew him now. This must be Mekiné's young brother Mairilek: no young Immortal, only an ordinary apprentice. She had been expecting him, she should have understood sooner.

He saluted her, and coming to the foot of the steps paused, looking up eagerly. There was a thin circle of blue beads about his strong smooth throat. Rahiké smiled and said, "Yes, I have it. You got my message?"

"Ah, thank you, Madam Rahiké! Yes, Mekiné told me I might come. What is it?"

His hands grasped the rails, his eyes were shining. She laughed. "How should I know? You must come up and look at it."

He sprang up the steps as she turned into the house. After a moment she looked out again; he was lingering on the porch, stroking his fingers along the carved rail, scrupulously not going beyond her invitation. His politeness pleased her. She said, "Come in, if you wish."

He stepped over the threshold then paused and looked around the room, looked with eyes that had been taught to see. His expression, first admiring, grew wistful. "I suppose," he said, "none but Masters would have worked on this house."

Burdal looked suspiciously round the doorjamb of her room. "Who's that?" she demanded. Rahiké, in the back room, did not answer, but the young man bowed and said respectfully "I am Mairilek, an apprentice of the Potter's Lodge, whose Master is Dairek, Miss Burdal."

She stared at him unappeased. Her mother emerged,

saying, "This is Naniel's uncle, Burdal, and don't be rude."
She held out a leather-cased object to the boy. "Here it is,
Mairilek; and I trust it is what you hoped for."

He took it in his hands and stood still, tense with
delight. He did not thank her, only raised his head and
looked his gratitude, breaking into shaky laughter. He was
altogether the charming boy of his reputation, and she
smiled kindly at him. "You had better sit down," she said,
doing so herself. He sat on the long bench, across the
room from her, and began unfastening the straps.

It would have been easy to have left the thing with
Mekiné, and if that had seemed a snub it would have been
only his due, for asking the Young Mistress to go on errands
for him. But as she discharged the commission she had
grown suspicious, curious to see him and his purchase
together. Now she had to admit that had she remembered
his face or not seen him in such a raw dawn, she would
have had another motive. Her attention was quite diverted
from the instrument, and curiosity lost in frank admiration.

To speak strictly, he had a fault, which was his hair.
By all the canons it should have been lighter, with a silky
curl; his was thick and heavy, and it waved rather than
curled. But Mairilek's beauty was of that order which
could transcend any rules, and looking at the glossy strength
of his hair the sternest connoisseur could not have wished
it otherwise. His eyes, lustrous and mild, were very dark,
and in the open sweetness of their smile Rahiké recognized
the bright-faced boy of years ago. But she could see the
child nowhere else, and this Mairilek did not move her to
the half-sisterly affection and scorn she remembered. His
was not the muskless beauty that delights the eye alone.
Rahiké looked at him with delight, acknowledging that
Mekiné had not exaggerated. Hiramarrek indeed: though
surely even Nehaté could not freeze such a summer. But
she was no longer a girl at the mercy of her blood, and its
heating could not overthrow her calm.

Mairilek had drawn off the leather cover and let it fall;
now he set the thing on his knees, resting his hands on it,

and gave a crooning sound. Rahiké smiled. To her it was
only a box strung with wires. It had four irregular sides,
the longest a little longer than Mairilek's hand and forearm,
and was about a handsbreadth deep. In itself it was
handsome, made of several kinds of wood polished and
inlaid, but she marveled that the youth should not grudge
giving all he had for it. Especially as she could see it was
almost as incomprehensible to him as to her. She watched,
amused, seeing how hesitantly his fingers moved over it,
and said, "I am surprised you were not more impatient to
fetch it, if it is so important."

He answered, "I would have been worse than a fool,
to come here the day you returned, and without permission.
Bad enough to have forced myself forward as I did—that
has kept me awake, without adding more impertinence.
Then I thought you would have callers—there must have
been many women wanting to hear about Halkal-Mari.
And I knew you had a little girl. I came as soon as I
dared."

His voice was lower than she had expected, and
stronger; she liked the lack of affectation with which he
spoke. He had none of the coquetry of her love, Rithakel,
who had been far less of a beauty. She almost asked why
he had not come straight from the Town, but checked; she
was not sure she wished him to know she had watched
him leaping along the hillside. He turned his attention
back to the box, feeling the strings gently. Burdal had
stolen out of her door. "What is it?" she asked. "What
does it do?"

He answered the child readily. "It is a music box," he
said. "It makes noises. Listen." He plucked one string,
then another, then another. The notes throbbed softly in
the air. Burdal opened her mouth and came nearer; he
glanced at her with a faint smile. When he plucked the
next string he frowned, and listened again; hesitated, then
cautiously touched something at the side of the box. The
note wailed oddly, up and down, a faint tickle in the ear,
and Burdal laughed. He smiled at her and plucked the

same string again, his fingers busy more confidently at the
edge of the instrument, until the sound satisfied him. One
by one he touched the strings, and they made a ladder of
sound, not quite regular, but pleasing.

"Let me!" said Burdal imperiously. "May I, may I do
it?" She touched the string at his nod, but the sound was
dull, and Mairilek showed her how to do it better. His
uncertainty was vanishing; his fingers moved delicately
but with assurance, his face grew calm. Watching him,
Rahiké thought, surprised, But he is a man! Why do we all
call him a boy? He is not a boy at all!

The thought made her shift uneasily. Beautiful boys
were a recognized part of the world, its best ornament;
but a beautiful man was something more incalculable.
Presently she said, "That is enough, Burdal." The child
looked up at Mairilek and he smiled, resting his arms
across the box so that all the notes died suddenly. "Perhaps
I can again?" she suggested, and he agreed. "Perhaps, one
day."

"Is it worth what you gave?" asked Rahiké when she
had shut the door on Burdal. "It took it all; or as near as
can be all. I did not know apprentices were so rich."

He looked up with a laugh, only the second time he
had looked directly at her since entering her house. He
was modest, she thought, but not as gauche as she had
been led to believe. His diffidence might be reserve just
as well as shyness.

"We are not. I won a bet, that is all; the best luck I
ever had." He ran his hands over the smooth wood again.
"Oh, it is worth it all, madam. I cannot tell you. I cannot
thank you enough."

"But I am still puzzled what use you can have for it.
What are you going to do with it?"

He did not answer at once, and kept his eyes bent
down. Then he said softly, "Learn its secret . . . I hope."
He touched the strings again, very gently, as if he felt life
beneath his fingers; and the smile he gave then was like
none she had seen on a man's face before. It had an

absorbed and tender joy, like a woman's smile over her baby. No, more secret and luminous even than that; like one who feels the child stir beneath her heart.

The Young Mistress drew in her breath, shocked. A sudden suspicion shook her. But all men delighted in what was strange and skillful. That was their nature, and their duty. She ought to allow him the last doubt.

She said, "In the Market Lodge where I bought that, there were many such things. I had to ask a craftsman to guide my choice. The making of them must be a great craft."

"Indeed it must be," he said, but quietly. He had seen the hook in her question. Then he went on, fumbling for each phrase. "Many such things—a Market Lodge— and a craft to make them— There must be many people who want them, then. But, maybe only women buy them—only women are permitted—do you know? Did you see any men who played upon such things?"

It was true, then. His tone confessed it. A musician: he wanted to be a musician! No wonder he was the despair of his mother and sisters. And she had allowed him to make her a helper in something not far short of disgraceful! She felt outrage at first, then a reluctant amusement. Had he meant to deceive her, or had he acted innocently, blinded by this obsession? In any case the fault was hers, for not being more cautious; if it had been something which concerned the City, how angry she would have been, how much to blame! A musician! How could she have guessed at such a thing? She knew people who could mark the beat for a song or dance, but the nearest Naramethé had to professional players were temple servants with their drums and rattles; and they were all women. What was the boy thinking of?

Yet, she could not help but pity him. The Craft Laws were men's mysteries, and no affair of hers, but she knew music was not a craft. And a man must be a craftsman. Such a passion as Mairilek's was folly: was worse: was dishonorable; and she saw the justice of the low esteem he suffered. Then he raised his eyes. Had she searched their depths she might have found shame, anger, defiance; but all Rahiké saw was their sadness. It was a strange look, full of a sorrow so unreproachful it seemed only patience. Like his voice making his admission, it waited to accept harshness; and her judgment was turned aside. She could not rebuke him. Instead, she answered his question.

"Indeed I did," she said gently. "They play in the presence of the Queen."

His eyes warmed; he smiled with a glow that heated her to her core. The gratitude in his look hurt her. "Did you see them there?" he asked.

She was glad to laugh. "Gracious Rehera! I was not her guest. No, I saw the Queen only for a moment, in audience with others like me. We were there to pay our respects, not to be entertained." She paused; she had lately talked so much about the wonders of Halkal-Mari. But everyone knew how greedy the Town was for news, and it was not easy for them to get it firsthand. Mairilek had a look that was interested without being expectant. After all, it was a safe topic, and maybe it would give him a little pleasant importance in his Lodge. So she talked of the southern city, and of the glimpsed glories of the court of the Queen among Queens, until it was time to light the lamps, and when she rose to do so, he rose also.

"I have stayed too long; your pardon, Madam Rahiké."

She shook her head. "No, you have been welcome." But she opened the door and led him out onto the porch. He went a little down the stairs before pausing again to speak; it was another courtesy which pleased her, his placing himself where she need not look up to him, for he was nearly a head the taller.

"I must thank you again, even though I grow boring; I will never have done thanking you."

She laughed and gestured deprecatingly, leaning on the rail to watch him go. Suddenly she called, "Mairilek!"

He turned and looked up. "When you have learned to play your music box a little, bring it here again. I would like to hear it."

His eyes widened, surprised and gratified. Then he gave her a sudden flashing smile and nodded, before walking on. She leaned there, rocking a little on her folded arms, thoughtful; then roused herself with a puzzled laugh, and turned back to the lamplit room.

Rahiké said, "Well, Mekiné, if I had guessed what it meant, maybe I would have refused in the first place. But how could I know? I knew you used to worry about him, but not why. I had a vague idea he wasn't very bright; not of anything like this. It isn't something that comes to mind!"

Mekiné stared unhappily across her courtyard. "That's true. Yes, I can see you wouldn't think to refuse when he asked you. But after? . . . You could have changed your mind."

"To be honest, Mekiné, I hardly thought about it. It was a big worry, you know, that journey. I know you think work never worries me, but it does. You can't just walk into Halkal-Mari and say, 'We want to register a new price for our incense'—you have to persuade them. And I'd never done anything half so important before. Until that was all over, I thought of nothing else much, except Burdal. It was only when I went to buy it; when I saw what was there, and when the craftsman asked me questions about the person who would play it. I couldn't give him the answers—I couldn't even understand the questions. *Then*, I began to wonder; but it was too late then." She leaned back against the porch post. "Don't be angry, Meké; I didn't mean to do any harm."

Her friend sighed. "No, you aren't to blame. I should have told you, perhaps. But we never liked to talk about it, outside the family. I thought the fewer to know the better. And it upsets my mother so much."

"The Town must know."

"Oh, of course . . . but that doesn't matter."

"What the Town knows the City hears in time."

"I don't think they would gossip about him. Why should they?"

"True; if I were a man—Rehera save me—I wouldn't want to remind women that Mairilek existed. Though I might want them to think poorly of him. He must rouse a good bit of jealousy."

Her friend looked at her with a sad half smile. "You don't think much of men, do you? I don't think he does. Tirek says he is quite well liked. Laughed at, but liked. *I* meant, men are loyal to each other."

They sat in silence for a while. The flowers growing before the porch smelled sweet, and the air was so still that the smoke from their pipes rose without a waver, twisting and plaiting, catching the sun on its blue slants. Spring had gone beyond the peril of night frosts, and the golden leaves of the incense bushes glowed in the late light. Her eyes straying back to her charges, Mekiné said, "You got the new price, anyway."

"Oh yes; or most of what we wanted." Rahiké waved her hand. "Not incense, Mekiné; talk about anything but that! I've had enough for a long while."

"No wonder you haven't called around lately."

"Yes, I'm sorry—nothing to do with the bushes. No, it's only that I've been helping a bit at the farm—Zoharé hasn't long before her time now, and she's been feeling a bit sluggish, her back's been giving her trouble too."

"Odd; she looks the strongest of the three of you, but she always seems to make heavy work of her pregnancies— not like you and Mirrik."

"Yes, it is strange. Anyway, that's where I've been. They have plenty of hired women, of course, but one more makes a difference, even when it's me. And I like it, if it isn't for too long. Especially since the heavy work is over now."

She rose and went to look in at the sleeping children,

Burdal among them. When she came back to the edge of the porch she said, "They have a Lodge in Halkal-Mari, you know. Musicians, I mean. Though they call it a Power, not a Craft—it doesn't rate as high. All the same, there is a Lodge, and Masters, and all the rest. So there are in a few other places, I understand."

"I had heard so. Mairilek had heard rumors. But even where there are such places, it isn't the same as a Craft. Anyway, what they have in Halkal-Mari makes no difference. This is Naramethé."

These days, Rahiké was rarely able to spend a whole evening with her friend; this was the first in the half-moon since she had come home. Her own work had become as great a barrier as Mekiné's lover. She thought, I spend too much time usefully now. Idle conversation had become a luxury to her, and she did not really care what the subject was. She would have talked as happily about dogs or the courtyard flowers, but if Mekiné wanted to unburden herself about her troublesome brother, she was content to listen.

"Has the box made much difference? To him, I suppose; but to what he would become? Would *not* having it make a potter of him? I know it's a pity to encourage him, but has no one ever done so? And he has not given up?"

The other woman shifted uneasily. "Not encouraged him. Never that. Not after we understood: but how could we, in the beginning? Maybe I did encourage him, when I was young. It was hard to blight him all the time. Perhaps my mother should have been sterner with him, though I really can't see how. But she is not a harsh person. And it was never easy to be harsh with Mairilek. He was always good tempered; whenever he was punished, he took it so sweetly.... You know how that can make it harder to be strict, stay firm; he was always so docile, it was hard to remember what he had done to be punished."

"No, I don't know. I never have that trouble with Burdal, alas," said Rahiké drily. It was good for a girl to be strong willed, but her daughter sometimes took it to excess. "What about his friends? Didn't they get him out of it? Well, obviously they didn't, but why not?"

"He didn't really have any. Not that he lacked company; he had lots of children to play with when he was a child, but they would try to order him about, him being so quiet. And however he may seem, he won't have that. He wouldn't quarrel—he never quarreled: he just went away." Mekiné's face grew troubled. "Now you make me think of it, he hasn't ever had a friend, not a close friend."

"It may be different now. Who knows how it is in the Lodges?"

"Yes; but I'd think he would have mentioned someone. He does talk about them, but no one specially, except the Master. It isn't as if he's disliked—just that nothing gets *through* to him. It was the same when we used to scold him. He was never defiant, he was always sorry, but nothing ever made a difference. He was like raw dough—he gave way easily, but sprang back when you stopped pressing."

Rahiké began to grin, then snorted with laughter. "To be honest, Meké, he sounds a lot like you. I'd as soon try to move a tree as to change your mind. If you've taken root in an idea—you don't fight, but you don't yield."

Mekiné smiled. "Maybe. After all, he *is* my brother. Though he does yield, or he seems to. But he was such an odd child, Rahiké. He used to chirp. Yes, but it wasn't funny then. He didn't talk, you know, until he was nearly four years old. And he never chattered to himself like other children, he'd just make noises—for hours at a time. Hee, hoo, doo, dum, hoo; even when we spoke to him. Often he only answered with his noises, until we shouted at him. My mother was often frantic with worry. I think she really feared he was half-witted, for a time. I mean, you've heard of children with birds in the head, but have you ever heard one *chirrup*?"

Rahiké listened smiling; Mekiné's tone of censure was

fading as love overcame her disapproval. Even pride was entering her voice. He was the youngest, the pet; she had always adored him.

"Then, when he got older, he was always finding new things to bang, or squeak. Very ingenious, some of them; and the noises he got out of them could be really clever. I couldn't help but be interested, sometimes; and then he would be so pleased. . . . I suppose I may even have praised him, now and then." She sighed. "Not that it made any difference, I suppose, praise or blame. And then, we didn't imagine the harm that would come of it. Plenty of peculiar children make quite ordinary adults. When he was a boy, you know, he sang so beautifully. The Mistress used to ask my mother to take him to sing to her."

"What about the men? Didn't he find any heroes, go through any passions?"

"No, not really; not like other boys. That did worry me. And when I began to hear that he didn't spend much time around the Lodges. He used to go over Nára, and we assumed he was in the Town like the others, hanging about the craftsmen. But no, he was off on his own. Not so much when he was very young, but at eleven, twelve; just when most boys get more interested."

"Was that when you began to doubt that he would grow out of it?"

"Out of what? We still hardly knew what 'it' was. We only wanted him to be ordinary. We still do. As if it isn't hard enough to be a man, without— And he did seem to be less odd as he grew up. To me, anyway. Probably, I was just seeing less of him, noticing less. I was getting older, had other things to think of. I never doubted that everything would be all right once he was an apprentice. I thought, when he had his Craft . . . and then I thought, as he got older there would be love affairs. I was only about nineteen—you know at that age you think love affairs will solve everything. But it didn't happen."

"Oh, come! No lovers? I don't believe it!"

"Yes, of course, but not—not what I expected, somehow.

After all, he is lovely. A few years ago, all the girls were after him: ask your Mirrik. But he is quite shy. If shy is the word. Maybe it was only that he was in a position to be very choosy. To tell you the truth, though it pleased him at first I think he didn't like the attention after a while."

"And now?"

"He has got past young girls, really. He is courted, but nothing seems to last long. Whether it is they, or he— He never talks about it."

She looked pensive. Rahiké said, "It doesn't really matter, does it? The point is, girls or women, brief or long, they haven't put the music out of his head." The shadow was creeping along the court toward them; the porch still had the sun, but soon it would grow cold, and she would have to go. She went on. "It never helps, telling someone not to worry; but I don't see there is anything you can do. Or could ever have done. And don't forget, he belongs to the Town now. He is answerable to his Master and his brothers, not to his mother and sisters. No comfort to you, I know."

Mekiné raised her hands and let them fall onto her thighs. "No, you're right. We can't do anything. Only nag, and wish, and keep discouraging him. Don't encourage him, Rahiké."

Rahiké leaned forward to knock out her pipe against the step. "Our Good Lady! It isn't in my power to do so; except for the box, which was in ignorance."

"But you are one of the Mothers of Naramethé. You are the Young Mistress. Of course what you say makes a difference. Besides, when he was a child he admired you a lot."

She laughed. "That was a long time ago. Meké, aren't you still being too careful? If he has reached this age without being daunted— Not every ill has a remedy. Voiha is sleeping, Mekiné. When she wakes—well, we shall see the world made right then. Till then we must bear it as it is."

Mekiné smiled sadly. "If nothing but Voiha's waking can help him, my poor brother!"

"Blasphemy! She may wake tomorrow!" But Rahiké laughed as she said it. All human life was only filling the break in time while the Dreamer slept, and when she woke the world would go on again. Rahiké believed it; but she was not ill pleased with the mortal makeshift, nor longing for the dream to end.

All the women of Naramethé shared through Meeting in the government of their land, but Rahiké had always known she needed more than that. She was clever, a girl who had stayed long at her studies, but no single kind of learning had drawn her. She was a weaver, not a spinner. Her delight was to see the pattern and the proper place of every thread in it, in planning how it might grow, in making something strong and harmonious out of diversity. From her girlhood she had wanted to be one of the Mothers of the People; she would have wanted it had she been her mother's heir and not the second daughter. One farm, one household would never have satisfied her appetite for authority. Yet ambitious as she was, she had not foreseen that the chief part in the work would be hers, that she would in time be the Mistress herself. It was still less than a year since her countrywomen had elected her to the succession, and time had not staled the marvel of it. The months since then had been comparable only to the first weeks of Burdal's life: every day of ceaseless care, hours of frustration and despair, but times also of exhilaration, and the whole utterly satisfying. With her daughter and her work, she was a happy woman; she, entirely happy, would have said.

She counted herself also fortunate that her rise to eminence had not estranged her from her sisters, a thing often heard of. Zoharé was like their mother, a farmer to her marrow, while Mirrik envied no one. Siké was too young to feel rivalry, only emulation. As for their mother, she was torn between pride and a reluctance to see any of her daughters leave the farm. She could not comprehend a preference for another life, and though Rahiké had left the family home at twenty to lodge in the City, not until her election had her mother believed she would not return.

The farm was a sprawling building of plastered brick, quite unlike Rahiké's neat wooden house. At its heart was the long room with porch before and yard behind that was the basis of all Halilaki houses, but around that center it had changed shape with every generation. The rooms where the sisters had slept as children were a herb garden now, only two courses of bricks marking their shape, and the present children had their bedrooms over the barns.

Most of the fields were west of the house; as Rahiké walked up from the City she passed between a field of oilberries and a pea field in bloom, but no one was working there. The house had been newly yellow-washed; Rahiké had seen that from the City, but she was amused at noticing a less expertly applied coat of color on the doghouse. She went into the house not really expecting to find anyone there; but Mirrik was seated before a table spread with papers.

"Burdal isn't here; Siké's taken her and one of the donkeys off somewhere."

"I didn't think she would be; didn't want her to be, she'd only think I'd come to fetch her home early, and then there'd be uproar. No, I only came for a walk and a chat, and to bring a cape for her to come home in. Where is everyone?"

"Zoharé is hoeing, mother's with the farrier, the aunt's with the short-hire women, I don't know about all the women. I, as you see, am bringing the books up to date."

"I'd have thought Zoharé would have sent you off with the hoe and sat down herself, the size she is now."

"Ah, but she wanted them done *right*. No, she's happier off on her own in a field; she's getting grumpy with herself, and she says as soon as she sits down she falls asleep. Do you want a drink? I'll make one when I've finished this."

"No hurry. Where's Thadek?"

"Asleep," said Mirrik, gesturing to the alcove by the hearth. "Don't wake him, he's being a beast."

"Teeth?"

"Huh: I wish I had such a handy excuse every time I was in a temper."

Rahiké grinned; Mirrik was a much better mother than she liked to appear. "The house looks good. Who smartened up the dogs?"

"Sinak, of course." They laughed. "What he found to impress him in the painters, I don't know. Two of the meekest little men I've ever seen. I don't think I heard ten words from them both all the time they were here. The aunt was the only one who could get them to open their mouths."

"If you mean you tied their tongues, I'm not a bit surprised. Well, Sinak's at that age, isn't he? Where is he now? With the girls?"

"Gracious no; they wouldn't have him. He went off with Mother and the farrier, but I saw him in the yard not long ago with some other boys. He's always getting chased away these days, poor child; too full of questions about things that don't concern him."

"Time he started going down to the Town."

"I expect he will soon." Mirrik turned her chair away from the table and smiled teasingly at Rahiké. "After all, if even *you* are taking an interest in it—"

"Me?" said Rahiké in genuine astonishment. She cast her mind about, thought of a Lodge petition that had been sent to her, and wondered how Mirrik knew of it. "You mean the appeal against the foresters? So, you are into the woodworkers' Lodges now, are you? This is new; what's his name?"

Mirrik chuckled. "I don't know anything about any appeal. No, I meant the beautiful potter."

"Oh!" It was days since her talk with Mekiné; Mairilek had been half forgotten. "I might have guessed you'd hear about that. Do you have the whole Town in your pocket?"

"By no means. Not him, for one; nor in anything else of mine, alas."

"I must say I didn't expect it to be so interesting to everyone."

"You didn't? The Town can't get over it. A dim-witted apprentice gets the Young Mistress running an errand for him all the way to Halkal-Mari! Not that *I* find it hard to account for; I think he must be pretty hard to say no to."

Rahiké laughed, feeling no need to discuss it seriously with Mirrik. "He couldn't ask much that you'd refuse, eh?"

"Not likely. The problem is, what can *I* ask that *he'll* refuse? Of course you wouldn't know, I suppose, that he's not much more than an errand boy in his Lodge?"

"Well, I'm certainly learning a lot about him. All I knew at the time was that he was civil and harmless and Mekiné's brother. An errand boy?"

"Holy Fire, I could find a few jobs for him!"

"Set him to work, would you? Wear him out in your service?"

Mirrik rolled her eyes and crowed. "What a lovely thought! He doesn't look as if he'd tire easily, either, does he? . . . . But Gracious Rehera, it would be fun to try!"

Rahiké laughed again, but felt strangely uneasy. "Enough," she said. "It's very well for you; you've always known him as an apprentice. But I keep thinking of Mekiné's baby brother."

"How unnerving. And what you've seen lately hasn't changed your picture?"

"Mirrik, I don't know what the talk of the Town is or what you've heard, but I've seen him *once*. Startling, I must admit, but not quite enough to root out what's been in my mind so long. Especially since I'm glad to say there's a lot of other things in my mind."

She ended with faint hauteur, and Mirrik regarded her with a half smile. "Dear sister, I often wonder why the Queen of Earth wasted a perfectly good body on you."

Rahiké was taken aback. *"Wasted?"*

"These last few years, yes."

"I'm very busy, that's all. And I've got Burdal."

"And I've got Thadek."

"That's different: you don't live alone with him." She felt quite ruffled, and was pleased that Thadek woke then to distract them. Mirrik said, "Hold him, will you? He's not wet. I'll make us a drink." Rahiké played with the child until his mother came back with the cups, then set him on the floor with a toy. She said amiably, "Well, no one could accuse you of waste. It's marvelous, really, you only have Thadek."

She was not really surprised; in Halilak, where men and women came together when the women chose, they usually bore their children at long intervals. In Naramethé a large family was something of a stigma, though there were places where the rich and idle bred freely.

"No marvel. I'm blessed with good rhythm, and my timing is very good. Are you saying I overindulge?"

"Certainly not. You don't make a fool of yourself. Of a few men, maybe."

"It's all prudence; I'm preparing for my middle years." Rahiké raised her brows, smiling, waiting for the joke, but Mirrik said quite coolly, "Times are good now; but when I'm *forty*-four? Don't forget I'm a farmer; in another twenty years I could be getting a bit leathery, couldn't I? It will be a good thing then, to know there are men with happy memories of me."

Rahiké had not thought her sister could still surprise her, but at that she stared dumbly, then broke out laughing: "And I'm supposed to be the one with foresight!"

"Probably it's like your maternal urge—you spend it all on Naramethé."

"Mirrik, there's no one like you."

"There is, then: what about mother? Didn't you know she pulled Sinak up from the same well as Zoharé?" Rahiké had not known. "There, a surprise for you. By the way, she said if you called to tell you to go to the fowl house for some eggs; if we send them down with Siké and Burdal you may not get them all. And Bohsa said to tell you, she's got some early vegetables she's pleased with."

Bohsa was one of the senior farm-workers, and her vegetable garden was an excellent one. Rahiké set off in search of her and her family as soon as she had finished her drink. Visits to the farm always lasted longer than she intended; it was nearly sunset when she left, leaving her barely time to prepare a meal for Burdal's return. She walked swiftly, gaining on a man ahead of her, until she recognized Mairilek. The memory of Mirrik's ribaldry made her drag her feet for a moment; then she shrugged and went on. When she came up with him she greeted him, saying, "Are you going to see Mekiné?"

"Yes, madam; but that is not why I came." He quickened his pace a little, to match hers. "My Master sent me with a delivery to one of the shrines. He finds me more use that way; more back than hands, he says. That is, I may not be skillful but I'm strong."

Rahiké glanced at him, then hastily away. He had spoken innocently, and she was disconcerted and annoyed by the coarseness of her response. Mairilek walked silent at her side, unconscious of her discomposure. Presently she said, "Greet Mekiné from me, and the children."

"I will." Then he said hesitantly, "Young Mistress: I am sorry if my sister blamed you for bring my music box."

"Oh, has she scolded you? No, don't worry, she didn't blame me. She told me about your childhood; how you used to worry them all by making noises instead of talking."

"So they tell me; I can't remember. I did play with the sounds, I remember that. I used to imitate what was said to me with noises. It got me into trouble often."

"Imitate with noises? What do you mean?"

He gave her a quick look, then uttered a series of sounds. They were not words, but in their pitch and timing she heard the shape of her speech. She stared at him, then laughed. He grinned, and repeated the notes of her laugh. She raised her hand, saying, "No more! I can see why it made trouble."

"Then if I found a sound I liked"—he repeated her laugh—"I would make it over and over, and play with the pattern. It must have been dreadful."

She allowed herself a small smile at the flattery, but made no comment, nor asked another question. She did not notice that her steps had slowed. He took a pipe from his belt, and began to blow upon it. The melody was sweet, and by degrees familiar; the second time he played it she recognized the song, though she could not have named the bird. She was impressed, and had to restrain praise. Instead she said, "So you have had something to play?"

"My pipes, yes. But I made them." He looked at the one he held, and sighed. "Karathek knows how many I have made. They get better, but—"

He stopped abruptly. Looking at him, she saw him flushed and frowning. Then he went on resolutely, declaring his shame.

"I am not clever with my hands," he said.

He spoke without bravado, but not like one who had ceased to feel the pain. Rahiké was moved. For a man of Halilak it was a humiliation as bitter as impotence, and harder to conceal; indeed, often they went together.

The courage with which he spoke touched her. She said, "Have you learned anything of your Halkal-Mari box yet?"

"A little. It will take me a long time, it is very complicated. But I know something."

"Well, don't forget you are to come and play it to us. I do not think we can wait for perfection, so when will you come? I would say tomorrow, but Mirrik will be there. You know my sister Mirrik?"

He looked confused. "Not well," he answered quickly. Then, "I could come the next evening."

"I will expect you, then. I warn you, Burdal will want to touch the box again."

He laughed, once again a shy boy. "She may do so and welcome. Thank you, Madam Rahiké: I will come then."

Though Rahiké had included Burdal in her invitation, she thought the child would have forgotten Mairilek and his music box, but Burdal remembered him very well. She appropriated him as her own visitor, and became very excited, insisting on wearing not only her best trousers but even the smock she put on for great occasions. Not for the first time, Rahiké regretted that her daughter had no uncles. As soon as Burdal was dressed she went to stand at the porch rail, her attention divided between her own fine appearance and the path; it was not long before her shriek of excitement called Rahiké to the door. Mairilek came sedately this time, weighted with the instrument; he had groomed himself as carefully as Burdal. He wore a blue kilt again, but a finer one, with an enamel belt, and as well as the string of blue beads had bracelets on his upper arms. There was a comb in his hair, and three blue flowers. This time Rahiké was prepared, and could keep her thoughts on a leash; but Burdal greeted him first, and for some while conversation was between him and the child.

Later, when Burdal had been put to bed and lay behind a closed door describing to Heffa how she had plucked the music box and made a tune—Mairilek had guided her fingers, and Rahiké suspected that he had helped call the strong sounds from the strings—they sat drinking thinned wine, while he continued to play with the box, and she watched him. As he had said, he had only begun to master its intricacies. They did not speak, for he concentrated too hard. He looked older when he was lost in his work, his face almost stern. Rahiké tried to remember how old he should be. An apprentice, but not a boy: twenty-two, twenty-three? He changed what he played to the tune of an old lullaby and began to sing it, slowly, as he found the notes; sometimes repeating a phrase to get it right. His voice was pleasing. Rahiké interrupted suddenly; "I ask nothing about your Lodge, Mairilek; but is it easy to practice there?"

He raised his head. She could not see the smudge of paint above his lashes, only the deepened brilliance of his eyes. The lamplight falling over his breast and arms took her by the throat. He answered, "No, it is not easy. There is nowhere quiet, and it is hard to be alone. There is usually something the others want me to join—a Games, or something. Most of the time I go out of the Town."

She nodded, her eyes on the rug, one hand tugging gently at her hair. There was an idea in her mind that she did not wholly approve of, and did not mean to voice. She thought, I would like to help him; but perhaps I ought not. And this could be folly. There are times I can no more look at him than at the sun: I would be mad to think I could see him here and want no more. I would have to be sure of myself. It would be unkind to offer help then ask a return. Her hair writhed through her fingers. But . . . it is so simple; no trouble; and it might help him. His time might not be all his own, though. Mekiné did not say he had a lover, but he might. Very likely. And he might misunderstand—I could look a fool. Better not to suggest it. So she was as astonished as he was, to hear herself say, "Come here and practice, if you wish."

She bit her mouth and frowned, then was glad after all, and looked at him. He looked surprised and doubtful, and she smiled wryly.

"Don't you trust me, Mairilek? Don't worry, there are no conditions. I shan't charge you rent." He flushed vividly; she chided herself, and said lightly, "Only to give you somewhere fairly undisturbed. Except for Burdal, of course. Not if it would offend anyone."

He said quickly, "No one if not you, Madam Rahiké.

But are you sure? It seems an intrusion. And when I practice—my playing is not good, but practice might really annoy you. The same thing again and again."

"Oh, goodness, I shall make you sit on the porch, and shut the windows!" She laughed at him. "As for being an intrusion, of course I shall tell you not to come if I expect a visitor; and if you grow too boring I shall set the dogs on you. You will not offend me, Mairilek. Come if you wish; and if you do not wish, don't come."

He bent his head to the instrument again, and brushed the strings softly. "Then I shall come," he said.

He did not stay long after that. When he had gone she unchained the dogs and let them run, while she sat smoking on the stairs, relaxed and cheerful: even when it occurred to her that she was hardly complying with Mekiné's request not to encourage him. She was certainly doing that. Mekiné might well be offended. All the same, when she recalled him saying, "No one if not you," she smiled.

II

From then on he came most evenings. She did not treat him as a guest. She went on with her work inside the house and he sat on the porch trying different patterns of sound; building stairways of notes and running down them. He had been right, it was often tedious. But at other times she listened curiously, trying to understand what he was doing; and occasionally, when he played a tune, she listened in simple pleasure.

After a while, she would bring him a drink when it grew late, and sit on the porch talking a little before he left. Once, when it got cool early, she called him into the house. He had seemed tense and high spirited that evening, full of talk; Rahiké could not afterwards recall what they had said, only that it had amused them very much. But she never forgot how it ended. She had ceased by that time to find his beauty so unnerving, and that night even felt able to tease him about it, saying, "But why has your music box no rival? Why is there no woman who claims a share in your evenings?" She spoke from the kitchen, so could not see his face, and he answered lightly, "You must have forgotten. I am known all over Naramethé for a fool."

"Ah, but such a beautiful fool!"

There was a pause: then he said, very short and dry, "I have never thought well of women who want beautiful fools."

The tone of it brought her to the door, and she looked at him, concerned, regretting her levity. His face was averted. Apology would not help, but she must let him know she had not been laughing at him—not really. She said soberly, "But Mairilek, you have never believed them? You don't think yourself a fool?"

When he looked at her, Rahiké found she had to command herself to meet his gaze steadily. She had not expected such a cool direct look; until now the gentle brilliance of his eyes had hidden from her the firmness of his mouth. He looked at her as if across a gulf, as if measuring its breadth, considering whether the attempt to cross it were worthwhile: and she faced him in suspense, bewildered at herself. She had never before feared a man's judgment, but she could not mistake her relief when his face relaxed into a smile, and he said, "No, of course I don't."

"Well, I am glad to hear it!" But she was glad to have to return to the stove; it was a moment that needed breaking. Relief was followed by a small glow of elation, as if a danger had been passed, a goal reached; but she knew, astonished, that she had been humbled. Very strangely, she did not resent it. When they were drinking she said in a voice still subdued, "Mairilek, I beg your pardon for making stupid remarks." She smiled wryly. "Impertinent remarks."

He laughed. The summer was back in his face, but she had seen another season look out of it, and would not forget. "Oh," he said, "and I yours, for taking offense. As for your question, I could as well turn it back on you."

She lifted her head and answered austerely, "I am too busy for such things."

"And so am I, Madam Rahiké."

He always called her Madam Rahiké, and with perfect ease, not as if he had to remember to do so, or as if he ever thought of her in any other way. It pleased her less as time passed, though when it irked her most she was most glad of it. Her resolve to make no advances to him was unchanged, indeed it was strengthened by pride, and at last by a fear of driving him away. But there were times it was harder than she had expected. His air of gentle submissiveness, however deceptive, could not but be exciting to so forceful a woman as she was. More and more often she longed to touch him, to feel how smooth and firm his muscular back would be, how his strong hair would spring in her hands. Then the calm civility of his "Madam" was sobering and salutary. For him to use her name without a title, for her to ask him to do so, would indeed be an advance in intimacy, and one she had no cause to think he desired. She was certain of his indifference to her as a woman. She too had been sought after, and knew the signs that invited approach too well to think that Mairilek ever showed them. Since to conceal attraction if he felt it would require a self-command she would not expect from any man, least of all one of his openness, she was sure he felt none. Indeed at times she doubted whether he cared much for the game, and wondered if to be so pursued in his boyhood might have given him a disgust for it all; though at other times she thought this only balm for her self-esteem. Certainly, if it were so, it would be sad.

Rahiké, like many Halilaki women, knew little of men. All the important relationships of life were with other women, or with children. Women were fellow citizens, rivals, neighbors, leaders, enemies, coworkers, friends; all legal ties were with women, and the bonds of home, of work, of duty. Men were creatures of a separate world, of the Town. Family affection was strong, but even the men of their own family did not live with them when childhood was past. They went away at fifteen, to lead a strange and secret life. Otherwise, women knew men only as lovers, and that was commonly a fleeting relationship, always an unequal one. When a man and woman loved, he was the moon to her sun, the echo to her song. Rahiké had as a young girl played at love like all others, flirting with new apprentices, and later in her girlhood, later than most, she had learned the pleasures of the body, filling several years with brief fierce passions. But she had known little of the men and boys she had made love to, nor cared to know more; she could not now recall them all. The only one she had known well was Rithakel, who had been her lover half a year, and even of him she remembered his faults, his petulance and jealousy, more clearly than what had pleased her for so long. Then she had become pregnant, and when Burdal was born she lost interest in men, absorbed in the real love of a woman's life. Her general feeling for men had long been one of kindly scorn. A brother might have taught her to think more highly of them, but her only brother was eight years old. She had never known before what it was to talk to a grown sensible man, and Mairilek's company pleased her more and more. Naturally his untaught mind could have neither the breadth nor the firmness of a woman's, but he was very far from foolish, and had insights of his own that often surprised her.

More than all else his single-mindedness intrigued her—his devotion to his secret craft. When she asked why he had chosen to enter the Potters' Lodge, he said, "Because of Master Dairek; I knew him, and knew he would take me. But it is a good Lodge for me. A lot of the other crafts would have spoiled my hands." Rahiké was amazed; she had often wondered how far he was aware of his beauty. He rarely used much adornment, though that might be awareness that he needed none. This show of vanity took her by surprise, until she saw that he was not looking at the backs of his hands but at the palms and fingers, feeling their flexibility and sensitivity protectively. "If I were working with stone or metal I would get them scarred and calloused—especially someone like me, who would stay with the rougher work. Clay I can clean off them. They wouldn't stay supple, either, if I were swinging a hammer. That's another thing with some—stoneyards, smithies; they dull the ears of the men working there."

She stared in wonder. "But, Mairilek, you were only a boy! You had thought this out then? So long ago?"

"No, of course not; it was luck, really. But when I was thirteen, some musicians came here. You probably remember. Until then, you know, I didn't really know what I was doing. It was only when I heard them that I understood myself. I asked one of them for advice." He smiled. "Just that—what should I do—what a question! I'm sure he was puzzled how to answer me, but he did tell me that—to take care of my hands." He looked at her, the amusement in his eyes increasing. "He didn't encourage me at all, Madam Rahiké. He told me if there was no custom of music here, I would be better off with a craft. And that I probably wasn't strong enough anyway, because music was not a craft but a Power; and as it's not natural for men to have Power, it is right it should be hard."

Rahiké smiled. It was indeed unnatural to link the idea of power with men, though this use of the word seemed to her less presumptuous than wry and sad. It was too preposterous to be blasphemous; it was only a daring joke. Power did not lie in the shaping of sound, which vanished in air. Power was what she was learning to exercise, working with the Mistress. It was what she began to wield herself, as the rods of authority passed to her; what she felt heating her blood the next day, as she contemplated the first Order ever to bear, beside the Seal of the Mistress, her own name. The Old Mistress, watching her successor's face, chuckled. "I can give it up," she said. "Will you be able to, I wonder? I mean to be out of this chair in a few years, sitting in the sun, spoiling my grandchildren. But I think you'll die behind the plough."

"I shan't mind that."

"Your successor might."

Rahiké said nothing. She read through another Order forbidding any further cutting of a certain tree in three of Naramethé's forests, and signed it carefully. The Mistress said cheerfully, "You will have Nité's name in the woodworkers' Lodges. I've had three petitions from different Lodge Masters, saying no other wood will do what *karom* does, they must have the timber. I've told them all it's your decision. I warn you: Nité's name."

"Only for a while, I expect. And the foresters will thank me. So will everyone who already has *karom* cabinets; think how the value will rise. And the next generation of Masters. No, I'll be overwhelmed with gratitude. Not that I've ever been scared of offending men yet."

"No, I never thought it. You care too little for what they think, if anything. Voiha dreamed two kinds of us, and not just for the making of children. Men can be worth listening to sometimes." She eyed the young woman with cheerful mockery. "Or is Tiridal's boy teaching you that?" Rahiké looked up sharply, and the Mistress cackled. "Oh, yes, I hear you keep a pet musician now, like the Queen among Queens. You certainly don't care who you upset! How long has the boy been weeping in your lap? Ho, he has fine eyes all right."

Rahiké drew another paper toward her. "As a matter of fact he is not a boy," she said coolly, "although there is no denying he has kept his looks. Nor does he weep. I have not heard him complain at all. He is very good-humored." But this calm only increased the old woman's amusement.

"Yes, they tell me he's quite a charmer," she said. "No sense, of course, and no skill with his hands. Or not for pottery. You may know of some."

Rahiké decided to ignore the innuendo. "No one could say he had no skill who heard him with that music box. As for charm, he has pleasant manners, if that is what you mean. Nor is he the fool I heard he was." She wrote her name and put the paper aside. Quite a charmer. Who said so? "I do care whom I offend, Mistress. Who is it? Mekiné was annoyed with me, but only for a time, not now. He harms no one, except maybe himself, by playing on my porch. I admit he interests me."

The Mistress sighed heavily. "Holy Fire, so he does me! If I were fifteen years younger, I'd give you a run for him!" She laughed again at Rahiké's tightened mouth, then sobered. "You offend the Town, Rahiké; and don't ever forget that you are going to rule them too. It does not please them to see the Young Mistress showing favor to one who flouts their laws. No, don't tell me he keeps all the forms, I don't doubt it, I don't know the dog but I know the kennel; and it isn't the point. The Town lives by the Crafts and the Lodges—they *live* by it, Rahiké—and then someone like him sets the whole thing at nothing; and you take him under your wing. Can't you see what an insult it seems to them, how you seem to slight their judgment of their own people? To be interfering in what is *theirs*?" Rahiké frowned, impressed, but stubborn. "But there, I can't blame you as they do. Fire of Maha, I suppose I encouraged him myself. Ten years or so ago, when I used to have him up here to sing—I don't know what to compare it to. Nothing mortal. Poor Tiridal, she never knew what to feel about it; half proud and half appalled. I used to wonder then what would become of him." She rocked her chair back and stared out into the courtyard. "Yes, I understand your wanting to help him, but there's little help he can have. Especially from the City. We can't make the Town have Lodges for these 'powers' or whatever they call them. It's none of our business. Well, I only hope we would pity the boy as much if he were plain."

Rahiké nodded musingly. "I wonder. You seem to be mistaken in one thing, though, Mistress. Mairilek only comes to sit on my porch and practice. I don't take him to bed."

But the Mistress snorted, let down her chair with a bang, and gave a loud ribald laugh. "The more fool you, then! Boys like that aren't made to be just looked at!"

Rahiké was silent with her for the rest of the day, which only made the old woman laugh at her more. "Come, don't quarrel with me, successor," she said at parting. "Oh, I know, some people keep their minds in their trousers, and I am a coarse old woman, and you are above such things. I know you are, my dear." She patted Rahiké's hand. "So are we all, until the chance comes."

The Young Mistress went home itchy with temper, and unable to account for it to her satisfaction. It was not the gossip. If she had cared for that, she would not have been what she was. Mairilek's visits would hardly go unremarked, and most people would make the natural inference. She did not know what irritated her so.

That evening she said lightly, "It seems we are giving the City something to talk about."

"And the Town too. I didn't expect anything else. They have to have something to amuse them in the long summer evenings."

She drummed her fingers on the porch rail. "Well, don't come if it bothers you."

"Why should it bother me? They have said worse things about me. But—but you, Madam Rahiké—that is different—"

"Oh," she said quickly, "I don't mean to take notice of such foolishness!"

"Yes," he agreed, "foolishness." Then they fell silent.

If she ever thought of telling him to come no more, there was Burdal to deter her, for the child adored him. She still insisted that it was to see her that he came, although often he did not arrive until she was asleep, and the evenings when he appeared before she went to bed were festivals to her. She would cling to him and talk to him, gazing worshipfully; it both diverted and exasperated Rahiké to see how Mairilek's frown was more effective against misbehavior than anything she could say. It was plain too that he was genuinely fond of Burdal. Watching them together Rahiké sometimes felt unreasonably vexed. She knew she was jealous, but she did not know of whom.

But when Burdal's fourth birthday came, she lost interest in Mairilek for a while. Now when she went to the Children's Court it was to the school and not the playrooms, and she was full of self-importance. Jostling for position among the other girls, establishing new friendships and rivalries left her little attention for other concerns. Especially for men; this step to maturity made her suddenly very aware of femininity and status, full of womanly pride. When Zoharé's baby, born at that time, proved a boy, she decided not to admire him; Rahiké was exasperated, but Zoharé was only amused, though her little girl was not and scowled furiously at her young cousin.

"Never mind that," said Zoharé. "Those two are never together but they quarrel. Here, take him: see if he gives you any ideas!"

Like the older women of the family, Zoharé thought it time Rahiké had another child; with the tiny baby in her arms, the Young Mistress had a moment of thinking so herself. Her mother was sure of it. "One is not enough, if the Goddess will give you more," she said firmly. "Burdal will suffer; you'll hold her too hard."

Her great-aunt said, "But have another girl. I don't know what your sisters are about, bringing us all these boys." She herself had five sons, and no daughters. "Boys are all grief," she said. "They don't bring children to sit around your table; they aren't there when you are old."

The baby drew Rahiké to the farm every evening for a while, and she did not know whether Mairilek came to her porch. There was one day she would have gone to her family even without the inducement of the child, she had such news to impart. She had less appetite for gossip than most of her people, but it would have choked her to contain this; as it was the road was too long, and she had to call on Mekiné on the way to share it. The family was gathered on the porch when she arrived. While Burdal told her grandmother of her day's doings Rahiké paid proper homage to the baby, though since Siké had got him into her arms there was little chance for another aunt that night; but Mirrik eyed her and said, "Leave him alone, your mind isn't on dandling tonight. Come on, you've got news; what is it?"

"News and plenty, and very shocking. You won't

believe it, but it's certainly true. Be thankful it doesn't concern Naramethé." They all grew alert, watching her while she found a seat. "An envoy from Temari came today. It was someone I'd never seen before. It should have been a woman called Sikané; you've probably heard me talk about her. Mirrik, last time she was here, didn't you call on me when she was in my house?"

Mirrik nodded. "Very hard and clever."

"Well, so we all thought. I didn't like her much, in a friendly way—nor I think did she like me, not that that matters; but I certainly admired her ability. No one could help being impressed. I thought she was the ablest woman I'd ever met, and the Old Mistress thought much the same, which counts for more. I said I'd be amazed if Sikané wasn't running Temari, under the Mistress, in less than five years. Well, I was right in a way—I'm amazed."

"Sick? Dead?" Though why should the death of a foreign woman they had never met be of interest? They watched her in eager suspense, but suddenly Rahiké no longer felt like making a game of it. The news was too dreadful, after all; even of a stranger.

"No, worse. She has left Temari. Gone."

That was startling enough; to leave the place of one's birth was appalling, almost unimaginable. Zoharé cried, "Gracious Rehera! What happened to make her do that?" They had notions of dreadful family tragedies—mother, sisters, children all burned in a house fire, and she unable to see the place, maybe—or of calamitous quarrels, but Mirrik was closest. "Disgrace!" she cried. "What did she do? Defile a Temple? Rob the Treasury? Suborn a Court?"

"No, she wasn't disgraced when she *left*. She went on a trade mission to a place called Hamékil. It's a long way off, nearly as far east as Halkal-Mari is south. A long way for direct trade, but it seems it's an interesting place, has no eastern neighbors and access, they say, to the sea— though I'm not sure what that's worth yet. But Sikané. Well, the mission was expected to last a long time, but she should have returned a month ago. Only instead of her they got a messenger, with a letter saying she wasn't coming, she was never coming." Rahiké cleared her throat. When it came to it, it was not easy to say, even of a woman one did not like. "It seems she has a lover in Hamékil, and she won't leave him."

They all gasped. No one spoke. Siké looked from face to face, absorbing their shock; the younger children stared at their mothers. After a while Rahiké said, "According to the new envoy, Sikané sent back her report with the letter. She said it was very good, very full, an excellent report, a—credit to her judgment—"

She covered her mouth, pressing back the hysterical laugh. Zoharé said heavily, "Spiced meat is one thing, this is another. Fire of Maha! It'll sour my milk!"

"I can't believe it," marveled Rahiké. "The future she had! What she could have done with her life! And now— what she has done!" She shuddered. Their great-aunt asked, "What of her family?"; and Mirrik, "Had she any children?"

"Yes," said Rahiké. "I don't know how many or how old, but the envoy said 'children.' No, she hasn't abandoned them, they're with her. Since it was to be such a long business, she took them too."

There was a general groan. Rahiké's mother said, "Better for them if she *had* abandoned them, poor little things! There must have been someone to take care of them. Someone more fit than such a mother! Exile and disgrace! To take them to it! Are they girls?"

But Rahiké did not know. "I couldn't ask any more questions; the poor envoy was ashamed herself, just to tell it. I hope she wasn't a relative; I didn't dare ask. Even the Old Mistress seemed to think the less said the better."

Mirrik opened her mouth, then changed her mind; it was too terrible a matter for jests. Zoharé said, "Do they know anything about the man?"

Rahiké shrugged. Of course the assumption was that he must be a beauty, something extraordinary, more beautiful than—but it might not be so. It was often hard to

understand other women's passions, impossible to account
for such madness as this. Mirrik said scornfully, "We know
what matters, I suppose, even if she could hardly put it in
a letter! I wonder how *he* enjoys being part of such a
scandal? And what she'll do if he leaves her?"

"I can't imagine," said Rahiké. "Not come back to
Temari, that's certain."

Siké, awed by the atmosphere, said tentatively, "What
will she do in this other place? I mean, what work?"

"Again, I can't imagine. Nothing fit for her, I suppose—
not for her *ability*, that is. They can hardly think any
better of her than we do, unless Hamékil is nothing like
other places. Clerking, maybe; copying." Sikané! Such a
woman, doing such work! That she of all women should so
throw away power, respect! But of what woman could it be
believed? Mekiné had been as disgusted as Mirrik.

Rahiké took Burdal home early, as soon as they had
eaten. The family could talk of nothing else, and she had
no more stomach for it; Zoharé was right—such scandal was
too strong to be spicy. It roused contempt and anger. To
sink so low, to give up work, esteem, ambition, for a man!
The disgrace touched them all as women. There could be
no forgiveness.

Burdal walked sedately with her mother, deeply
impressed with it all. Presently she said gravely, "That
person you were all talking about was very bad, wasn't
she?"

"Yes, I'm afraid she was."

"Women mustn't do that, must they? Leave their
house and their friends and everything, just to be with a
man?"

"She left her work, Burdal. Women must not leave
their work for anything; for a man or anything else."

"Isn't anything as important as work?"

"Only children. And women don't leave work for their
children; it's their children really they do their work for.
You see, Burdal, Rehera gave us the job of looking after
the world; so to leave our work is very, very wrong."

Burdal fell silent again, pondering. After a while she said seriously, "*I* shall do *my* work. I think Aunt Mirrik is quite right about men: they're a lot of fun, but only for a game."

Rahiké gasped, then choked back her laugh; she ought not weaken the impression made on the child. So she said equally seriously, "I think she's right too," and led her daughter home.

Spring had become summer, but suddenly they had a few days of stormy wet weather; bad enough it seemed to prevent Mairilek walking from the Town, for the porch was empty for several evenings. Rahiké missed him, and hoped he had not taken her recent absences as a hint to stay away in future. She had come to depend on an hour of conversation to end the day, and the evening seemed flat after Burdal had gone to bed. Then came a day which promised a fine evening, until at sunset the clouds clumped again, and the rain began. Rahiké had just put Burdal to bed and gone out onto the porch; the evening was worth a look. The low sun still shone brightly, and the rain sparkled as it fell. The earth glowed under the dark sky. Before her a great rainbow stood over the valley, capturing shining air within it; and out from its arch came Mairilek, running through the bright rain.

The sunset gleamed with new brilliance. Rahiké leaned against the rail, struggling with an unseemly joy that urged her to call out, to run down the steps. The dogs barked wildly, but she governed herself. He bounded up the stair and looked at her laughing. His thick hair glittered with rain, his hard supple body was wet and gleaming. "Where is your cloak?" Rahiké asked severely.

"I thought I would get here dry."

"I'll get a towel. You had best come inside tonight, this will beat onto the porch."

He followed her in. She fetched a cloth, feeling stupefied, as if confronted by a disaster she should have foreseen, averted. Watching him toweling his hair and back she had a feeling as of standing on a riverbank and feeling it crumble beneath her. Yet her voice was steady. "It will take a fire to dry you; this is an evening for one, anyway." His hair was in a tumult, and he ran his hands through it, trying to smooth it. She had again the giddy sense of depths below her.

At that Burdal, not yet asleep, realized that Mairilek was there and scampered out to him. He turned to welcome her, stretching out his arm, his smile vivid with pleasure. Rahiké set a hand on the back of her chair. Her hold on the world broke, the void received her. The child leaned on Mairilek's leg and scrambled onto the seat beside him, putting up a hand to his untidy hair, while he looked down at her all attention and delight. For them time went on unbroken; but a flood had taken Rahiké, and cast her up on a strange shore.

She loosed her hold on the chair and walked carefully to the hearth, where she knelt, and took wood and kindling. Each simple action needed an effort of memory and organization. She heard Burdal say to him, "Your hair's wet," and to her, "Why have you let him come inside? Is he staying here?" and she replied, without turning, "It's cold and wet outside; you look, and see the rain." The flames that rose on the hearth rose also about her heart, and their smoke burned her eyes. For a while she stayed kneeling there, listening to the voices behind her, her eyes on the mounting fire. When it was burning strongly she went into the kitchen to clean her hands: and found she was afraid to go back to the main room. She leaned her hands against the shelf where the images of the little household deities stood, and every goddess seemed to grin at her with the face of the Old Mistress, until she laughed faintly. "You are a coarse old woman," she whispered. "And you are wrong: I fear you are wrong. It is not what you think. It is far worse than that. I am afraid it is love. Oh, I never felt this before. He terrifies me. It must be love."

She looked to the greater goddesses on the shelf above; but there was no image there of Karinané the Dancer, Queen of Birds, Mistress of Fire. If she had brought the Goddess of Love into her house and honored her, would she now have forced an entry and struck her to her knees? She had not known the power she slighted. What face would the Kindler now show her, one of kindness or wrath? "Great Lady, Flame-crowned, forgive my folly!" she prayed; but she knew that though there is mercy for sins, there is none for mistakes.

She went back to the room, and saw Burdal trying to speak through an enormous yawn. She smiled. "That's enough, Burdal. Back to bed. Mairilek has work to do." He turned to her, but she dared not look at him; she had become a fountain of fire, and feared her eyes must be full of the smoke of her burning. Burdal slipped to the floor without protest, and turned back to be kissed. She always did so, and Rahiké usually felt only approval. Now she was pierced, and her sight dazzled. If it had not been for the child she must have gone to him then; but the child was there, and the moment passed.

When she had settled Burdal again Rahiké went out onto the porch, to slide the panes of oiled cloth across the windows, and to bring up the little dog. She lingered there, though the glory of the evening had waned and the rain fell more steadily; it had become necessary to nerve herself for his presence. Behind her the familiar sounds began, his fingers running up and down the slopes of sound that always began his practice. The dog licked her hand, yawned, and scuffled into a comfortable corner. She rose and walked in. The notes rose and fell in a broken sequence, then began to shift into a more complicated pattern; he watched his hands, intent and frowning. She moved about the kitchen listening; but sometimes she stood still, feeling her spine sing to the note he played, and then all the goddesses cackled softly on their shelf.

He played more than usual that evening, and they talked less: Rahiké had only one thing to say, and was intent on not saying it. The music seemed to enclose him in its sweetness, building a wall behind which he sat unapproachable. The sunset died, the fire brightened; she lit the lamps and fastened the orange blinds. He rested from the strings and played his pipe. Whenever there was silence, they heard the rain. Rahiké went once to look at Burdal, then returning went to kneel before the hearth. The music had stopped; he watched her, his pipe idle in his fingers, while she gazed at the flames and felt their dancing in her head. The silence lengthened. Soon he must remark on it, say he must go. Panic forced speech from her. She said hastily, "That last tune on your music box, I liked that. Play that again."

After a moment he picked up the instrument. "I didn't play it well," he said, but he began. She rose and looked at her chair, then went to sit on the bench near him. She leaned there gazing at him, at his grave mouth, the dark crescents against his cheeks, his lustrous hair, and knew she had reached the end of striving. But she dared not interrupt him. He played on, sometimes hesitantly, sometimes fluently, altogether absorbed: the music rose like smoke between them. Far back in her mind, a small dispassionate voice said, It's so long since you did this, you've forgotten how. Promptly an answer came, I never did this before. She gave a tiny gasp, of laughter maybe, stifled at once; but Mairilek stopped playing instantly. "Yes, it is bad," he said; then, when she made no answer, no sound, "I'll try again." He moved to touch the strings; she stretched out a hand and laid it across them saying, "No."

He gave her a quick glance, and put the box aside. "You're right; there were too many false notes," he said. He looked at her, and this time she did not evade his eyes. They were bright and uncertain at first, but they softened as she watched as if clouded from within. She gazed at him in wonder, and said, "I didn't hear any."

"Then you were not listening, Madam Rahiké."

His voice was teasing and gentle; she felt the bench

sinking away from her. "Don't," she said. "Please, Mairilek, don't call me that."

"As you wish. What shall I call you?" And all at once he was imploring. "Tell me," he begged; "tell me what I should do?"

"Oh," she said, and put her arms around him.

He laughed then, moving smoothly into her embrace. His cheek was rough, a man's shaven cheek, not smooth like a boy's, and his hair had the live spring she had imagined; but she had not thought to find such strength in his arms, nor such heat in his kisses. When they drew back and looked at each other, she saw the tender gaiety in his eyes, but hers were filled with a darker passion and she could not smile. His eyes moved; he reached to push back her headcloth; she leaned her forehead on his shoulder. She felt his strong fingers in her loosened hair, heard the rain's faint patter, and clutched at him. "It's still raining. You can't go back, you can't go back."

"I never wanted to," he said.

Burdal woke in the night and set up the dull uncertain wail of a child disturbed without knowing why. Rahiké started up, confused for a moment by the weight that hampered her, the unquenched lamps. Mairilek stirred and spoke as she got up, but she did not pause to answer. Heffa was sniffing noisily under the door; when she opened it he thrust his shoulders out and gave one minatory bark. Burdal was sitting up. "It isn't dark!" she said.

"I'm sorry, I forgot."

"Who is here?"

"Mairilek," she said, and smiled to see her daughter's face clear. "Hush, or you'll wake him."

"Is he sleeping here, then?"

"Yes, he is tonight."

"And tomorrow?"

"Maybe. Lie down. I'll make it dark now."

The child allowed herself to be settled, reaching out her hand to find Heffa. "Will I see Mairilek in the morning?"

"No, he will be gone when you wake up. Tomorrow night, I expect. Go to sleep now."

Mairilek leaned up as she quenched the lamps, asking, "Is she all right?"

"Charmed by your name. You have two lovers in this house."

He chuckled. "I was sure of Burdal. I only wish you had been as demonstrative." She kneeled by the bed and smiled at him; they looked at each other, shy, exultant. He said, "I am glad to hear I might be here tomorrow."

"What will the other apprentices say to you?"

"Nothing, I expect. They'll be too busy settling bets. It should take them a long time; you really upset the odds." He touched her face wonderingly. "I can't believe I am here. I thought you would never ask."

"Oh, Mairilek! It was only that I thought you did not want me. I was afraid I would drive you away."

He sighed. "Have I convinced you yet? Shall I try again? Come closer."

Rahiké had work that took her out of the City the next day, and she was glad of it. She did not wish to curb her happiness, to bring her spirit down from the wing. Sober work at her desk would not have suited her mood as did taking a pony and riding to some of the public farmlands. It was a day of fitful sun, but to her it was cloudless, and the valley of Naramethé in its full summer beauty had never seemed so paradisal. Occasionally even as she talked business some image of Mairilek would come between her and the woman to whom she was talking, so that she found herself smiling inappropriately, and as she rode about he was never out of her mind. She was not a very skillful rider; few City women were, not good enough to be so inattentive; but that day she could do nothing amiss, and even the pony was kind to her. Only once was she almost sobered; one woman, thinking the Young Mistress's radiance could have only one cause, said that surely she should not be riding if she were pregnant. It was a thing she had not considered, not thought of dates and probabilities at all; conception could not seem desirable when it would part her from Mairilek. At the next shrine, she tethered the pony and struck the cymbal. It was a small place, with only one priestess who came hurrying from her garden with the hem of her long skirt pulled through her belt at the front; priestesses still wore the antique dress. Rahiké took a cheese given her by some herdswomen, and went in, but when the priestess came with hands washed and clothes rearranged, and asked to whom she was offering, Rahiké hesitated. She had meant to pray to Great Rehera and to Veraha the Womb-Filler, but it was impious, ungrateful, wrong, to pray to be spared a blessing. So she gave her gift to the priestess saying, "To Great Rehera and to Karinané; a thank-offering."

The day went by on wings of light and fire, and Mairilek waited at the end of it: and it was only the first of such days. Once, the end of work had been the end of living, and silence had fallen when Burdal slept. Already he had changed that; now he transformed all else for her, and she saw the world as Voiha might have dreamed it. Rahiké had not known that she was lonely. Her way had parted from her family's, her friends had grown fewer as she rose in authority, but she had Burdal and her work; she had not thought anything else needed to complete life. She had called her evenings restful; that they had only been empty, and her nights had been wasted in solitude. For the first time she knew it, now when together they filled every hour of evening and night. She had believed it was her nature to be sober and composed, when she had only lacked opportunity to be otherwise. In those days she discovered a gaiety in herself she had never guessed at, and life with Mairilek to share it became all honey and wine.

It was some time before the City understood that the Young Mistress was not merely amusing herself with a boy whose appeal all could see, but that she had taken a lover. When it was realized, what had been a subject for merriment became matter for scandal. A month should have ended the interlude, and it did not. Instead, they seemed to spend more time together. He was seen playing with her little girl, exercising her dogs; several people saw her sitting on her porch with him with her hair uncovered. The difference in their standing made the association grotesque. She was the Young Misstress, he was not even a respectable apprentice; in the scales in which men were weighed he was a feather, with nothing but his face to recommend him, and Rahiké was censured for making a fool of herself.

In the past she had herself feared that a lover might distract her from her work, but it was not so. She brought a new vigor to it, as to all her life; and the Old Mistress, who knew this, was her firmest supporter. To her successor she made little comment, beyond adding, "And how's the lovely boy?" to her daily greeting; but if she heard her criticized, she answered tartly that if Rahiké was a fool, it was a pity they could not all make such fools of themselves. It was Rahiké's mother who could not contain her distress; she upbraided her daughter, and they quarreled. This shocked them both so, besides frightening Burdal, that they made peace as quickly as possible; but it had startled all the family to see how fiercely she would defend her lover, even against her mother. Indeed, Rahiké herself was unnerved by her passion, and left overwrought; when Mirrik said to her, "It seems this is more important than I thought," she snapped back, "I daresay: most things are!" Then she felt ashamed, although Mirrik only looked amused, and said, "Why, what did you think?"

"Oh, you know; that if you've decided to enjoy yourself for a while it's a good thing and high time, and you couldn't have chosen a better playmate, I'm sure." She gave her sister another amused look, and went on. "Now Zoharé thinks because Burdal is four, obviously you want another baby, and she's glad you've learned from her example: also that you've picked a good man for the job. We're both agreed that there's no law that says the Young Mistress must choose her lovers by rank and not looks. Mind you, we also agree that there's no law either that says you have to do your courting in public; though it's hard to see what choice you have about that, being who you are and living where you do."

There was no use, Rahiké knew, in feeling angry; naturally they would suppose she was captivated by his beauty. What else did she want them to think? Any other distinction he had was no credit to him. She could only say, "I'm not ashamed of him, and I won't act as if I were!"

"Ashamed of him! I should think not. I think he's the most delicious thing on two legs, and I'm sure he's even better lying down!"

Such sympathy was not much more congenial to her than her mother's disapproval, her scorn of Mairilek. Rahiké was shaken. Gossip she had not minded, even censure, but to find her family blaming her with the rest hurt her almost to tears. She was in low spirits all evening. Yet when Mairilek coaxed the reason out of her that night he did not seem angry for himself, only for her, and he was as touched by her resentment as if he had not expected it. When she protested against such calm he said, "Why should I care what they think of me? You are not ashamed of me. It is only what you think that matters."

She gazed at him, perplexed, wondering if it were humility or security that made him so tranquil. There was so much to learn of him. She began to feel it would take a lifetime to know him, and she would not grudge a day of it. "And does it really not hurt you?"

He smiled at her. "How can it? Nothing can hurt me now."

His serenity soothed her indignation, but nothing could remove it. One evening she stood watching him, intent on his instrument, unaware even of her, striving hard against his ignorance, and she thought, But he is a craftsman; surely he is . . . even without a Lodge, a Master; it is hard to be his own apprentice.

He had been working at the same few sounds for some time; now he let his hands fall hopelessly onto the wood of the box. She said, "Is it very hard, Mairilek?"

"Oh, I shall get it right. I have before." He pushed his hair behind his ears and flexed his fingers.

"I didn't mean that, especially. I meant all of this. Music. I'm amazed sometimes that you have kept at it."

He glanced up at her, then looked pensively before him. "It is not quite like that. I have longed, sometimes, to be free of it—to be a craftsman—I have envied my brothers so. But *it* keeps at *me*. It will speak." He gave her his sudden enchanting smile. "When you carried Burdal, suppose someone had said to you, 'This is hard, how do you keep at it?'" He laughed at her reproving face. "Well, but it is like that, I am sure it is. Did you never weary of the burden, long to be free of it? But only by having her safely born."

She said severely, "You should not be talking like this." And she took the box from him, but only to make room for herself. He laughed again.

"If I were so shameless I might even ask you if your daughter did not cost you some pain."

"You are shameless enough for anything. No more," she said; for he was getting near sacrilege.

They were together less than was reported, though as often as they could be. Many things might keep them apart. In the days of her bleeding she must avoid the company of men; he could not come then. And there were other calls, of work or her family, on her time; and often there were ceremonies of his Lodge, or some event in the Town, to keep him away. Burdal grieved bitterly at such times. She understood about "tribute days" (so called because then Veraha took toll of unfruitful wombs) but could not see what else could keep him from them. On one such evening she hung disconsolately on the porch rail, demanding, "*Why* isn't Mairilek coming here tonight?"

"Because they have a Games in the Town and he has to be there."

"Why can't he come here instead?"

"Because all the men have to go."

"Wouldn't he rather come here than see a Games?"

"Perhaps. But I expect he enjoys them; men do."

"Why do they?"

"I don't know; I'm not a man."

"After it's over, will he come here then?"

"Not tonight."

"Why not?"

It was disturbing, the way the child uttered her own stifled thoughts. She said crisply, "Because he does not live here."

"Why not?"

"Because men don't live in houses."

"Why not?"

Rahiké was in no mood for that game. "Now you're being silly, Burdal. You know men don't live with us. They live in the Town. Sinak will go there to live when he is older, so will Naniel. All boys go there when they grow up. Mairilek lives with the other men." She rose and went into the house. Outside Burdal cried loudly, "Sinak says he is my uncle, but he isn't! He's only a little boy! Mairilek is my uncle! I told Grandmother, 'Sinak isn't my uncle, Mairilek is my uncle!'" Rahiké winced; she had heard of that. The child's voice settled into a defiant incantation, conjuring a more desirable world, one where she was stronger, Mairilek never absent, and all who parted them or criticized him were suitably punished. Her mother listened, in annoyance first, then growing appreciation, beginning to smile at finding herself in such sympathy. This vent for Burdal's temper soothed her own mood also, melting it into amusement. Burdal heard her laugh and was not pleased. She raised her voice. "And he will *sleep* here, and all his *clothes* will be here, and he will have his *breakfast* here, and he will have his *dinner* here, and—" She broke off as her mother appeared in the doorway, and stared at her with the truculence that always brought Rithakel before her eyes.

"Stop that at once!" said Rahiké sternly. "And don't let me hear you say such things again! If Mairilek heard you he would be *very* angry. He is not a little boy. Only little boys eat with women and only little boys live in houses. Now stop sulking. Come in and play with your toys."

But Burdal put her head down, ran into her own room, and slammed the door. Rahiké let her go and sat down with a sigh. The place where his Halkal-Mari box stood was empty; he did not mean to miss his practice when he was absent from her. One of his bracelets lay there, and she picked it up, ashamed of the comfort it gave her. She heard Burdal sobbing and sighed again. She was as miserable as the child, and she despised herself for it. It was weak, unwomanly, to miss a man so. The love of men was sweet, but it was the wine at life's feast and not the food.

Rahiké had a nature for love, though not one to come to it with Mairilek's blithe ease and grace. She was a strong woman, intense in all she did: she took many things gaily, none lightly. Yet she was also used to command, prizing her dignity, her judgment, her self-control; and she half feared this new kind of love which threatened to take her soul out of her own grasp. When Mairilek was with her all such thoughts were forgotten, but they returned in his absence and made it doubly dark. The lovers of her girlhood had touched nothing but her body; she had never been in love before, and had hardly begun to know what it meant. All her habits of thought joined to deny its power. Love was maternal love, the love which stayed, the love for which women were made. Men were here-and-gone creatures, and their love was a light thing, ornament and not substance. Rahiké had always believed it, she believed it still; and so she regarded her desolation when Mairilek was away from her as foolish and blamable.

In bed with him she found all the bliss she had looked for, and much more. She had gone to the spring of joy to drink, but she had drowned. It did not surprise her to think that she had lived so long without this delight; the difficulty was to recall that there had been any other times. As the plough goes over the fields and leaves behind no traces of past harvests, so with this love. She had known before the rapture which belongs to the flesh alone and neither gives nor demands more, but always her soul had held aloof. It did so no longer. Now she felt the passion that takes all and fills all, a fire in whose heat even desire melted. She delighted in his body, she rejoiced in her own that could please him so much; but the act was now means not end, not the whole of love but only the expression of it. At times she was awed by the joy they gave each other, for she had not guessed there were such depths in life. Those who have seen no glory greater than moonlight, how should they dream the sun may rise?

Outside the gate of the Court of Assembly was the hubbub of the markets under the fierce beating of the late summer sun, but within it was quieter, and a little less hot. The great courtyard was full of women come to admire the creations of the Town that were displayed there. Mirrik paused beside Rahiké. "You have been looking at that vase a long time, is there something special about it?" She was carrying her son on her arm, making him gaze at the artifacts, although he was too young to be edified by them.

"It isn't the vase, it's the bowl beside it," answered her sister. "Mairilek tells me there is. His Master made it. I said I would look at it." They gazed at the bowl together for a few moments, but the Potter's Booth now stood in the full glare of the sun, and soon Mirrik moved away.

"Don't be too long, if we're looking round the Market. It's near noon, it will be too hot for Thadek soon. I'm going to look at the weaving. Don't forget to see Tirek's work, or Mekiné will never forgive you."

Rahiké nodded, and stared at the blue bowl again. It was a handsome vessel, but so were the others; only the work of Masters stood there, waiting to be taken into the temple of Karathek the Hundred-Handed. Each year every Master sent his finest piece to the God, and for three days they stood in the Court of Assembly for all to see. Rahiké looked from bowl to bowl, trying to compare them for symmetry of form and beauty of decoration; then she gave up, and strolled after Mirrik. At least she would be able to describe it, and maybe he would forget to ask after it.

But it was the first thing he did say that evening, hardly pausing for an embrace before asking eagerly, "Did you see the bowl?" If her praise was, as she feared, more warm than discriminating, he did not seem to notice. "Oh, it is the best thing Master Dairek has done!" he cried. She was surprised and touched by his enthusiasm, which spoke such loyalty to his Master. "The vase beside it was a fine piece too," she said.

"Yes. That was Sadik's Master-piece. We have only one craftsman made Master this year, but I do not think there can often have been a better." He began to describe to her other works, and she watched him, increasingly entertained. She was surprised by the amount of craft knowledge he showed, but much more by his animation. She had thought his affection only for Dairek, of whose kindness to his incompetence he often spoke, but it seemed it was wider. Interrupting some esthetic point that she had not been heeding, she said, "Why, Mairilek! I thought you didn't care for pottery!"

He stopped, staring at her; a faint look of disappointment came into his face. "Not to make it. No."

She laughed. "No one would think so, to hear you then!"

"I was describing Sadik's wine flask. I was trying to make you see it."

"I would rather see you," she said, amused and tender; but he did not respond.

"You mean you weren't listening. Or you were taking no notice."

"Of course I was taking notice. Of you; you're more interesting than pots. I noticed that you were talking like a Master!"

He looked at her strangely, then sat down. "I will never be a Master, Rahiké," he said coolly; "I don't think I shall ever be a craftsman. But I know what good work is; and what it is worth."

"Well, and so do I," she began, but he burst out fiercely, "No you don't! None of you do! Not one woman in a hundred! To hear them talk in the Court yesterday—but I thought *you* would be different. I have never known a woman who ever bothered to *look* at anything!"

She gripped her chair, staring, between shock and anger. "What are you talking about?" She knew by now that he could be stubborn, but this show of temper was something new. He looked about, then jumped up and seized a small chest from the shelf where it stood.

"Look at this, then. You bought it, so I suppose you think you admired it, but I don't think so. I've never seen you look at it, or hold it: you stand it in a corner, and when I said how lovely it was, you only said it was useful for 'bits and pieces.' Bits and pieces! Have you looked at the carving, at how those edges are shaped, at the way it's lined, at the joints? At the carving, maybe, a little; not the rest. The only other thing I ever heard you say about it was some joke about it being *karom* wood and worth more now. It took some craftsman days—weeks maybe—to make that; and you grudge an hour to really look at it, though it deserves half a day. Yet you say you like wood carving!" He restored the box to its place, saying scornfully, "You women are so busy looking ahead, you never see what is before you!"

Rahiké grew pale, and her tawny eyes glittered. "It is as well we do! Since you mention *karom,* what shall we say about craftsmen so busy staring before them, staring at their own work, they never see they are leaving nothing for their own apprentices?" She clenched her hands, struggling with her anger; she rarely lost her temper, and to find herself doing so made her more furious with him. He looked stubborn, but did not answer: she remembered Mekiné saying, "He never quarreled, he just went away," and tasted terror. "As for spending half a day *looking* at something—or even an hour—how should I have so much time to spare?"

She turned away into the kitchen; where she had nothing to do, and had to contrive some activity. How dared he speak so, when she was trying to be interested in his concerns! She had learned already that he was loyal to his Lodge; but she had thought it only the loyalty of duty. Did he love her less than the Town, then? The worst of her anger was with herself for being so hurt; it was abject of her to care so much for a man's opinion. Was she to be at his mercy? Make him Mistress?

"Rahiké," he said from the door behind her. She did not look at him. Why should he attack her on behalf of the craftsmen? She had taken his part against the Town, now he took theirs against her. He came nearer. "Rahiké!" His voice was soft and beseeching. She would not turn.

"Why aren't you practicing?"

"Because you are angry with me. It locks up my soul." He slipped his arms round her, bending his face to her hair. "Don't be angry with me."

He had not apologized. She ought not relent until he apologized; but helpless as his music box she sounded the note he chose. After a moment she leaned back against him. "Well: but don't bite my hand so hard again."

"Never. All my life I will lie at your feet and lick your fingers." His words were meek, but his voice was confident. Overcome by relief, as if she had received forgiveness and not given it, she rested her head on his shoulder. He lipped her cheek, then said, "And the woodworkers don't blame you now for the wood."

Because she had upheld them in a dispute with the market traders, no doubt. She gave a faint chuckle; several scathing remarks lay on her tongue, but she swallowed them all and said without irony, "I am glad of that."

Late that night Rahiké lay awake and gazed at his face across their mingled hair. He looked calm and happy, and immeasurably remote in sleep. She thought, Will I always misunderstand him, always miscalculate? How long will it take me to learn him? He stirred, murmuring, his hand groping toward her, and she took it. He opened his eyes and smiled at her, blissful. At such moments joy had an edge as sharp as pain. He shook the hair back from his face and said, "You look very serious. What are you thinking?"

"About you."

His eyes glinted. "Well, of course!"

Rahiké laughed. She said, "I'm not usually stupid; why does my judgment always fail me with you? I never guessed you cared so much for the crafts."

"Why should I not? I am a man."

She turned over and leaned on her elbows, looking at him baffled. "They refuse you *your* craft, they oppress your life—aren't you bitter? Why are you not bitter?"

He smiled a little sadly. "Why; what use would that be?"

"Use! None, maybe. It would just seem natural."

He lay stroking her gently and did not answer at once. At last he said, "No one is to blame. The Laws are the Laws."

"Well, *I* should be bitter," she asserted. "I should storm, and rail, and accuse the Goddesses, and attack the Laws."

He laughed, tugging softly at her hair. "I am sure you would. You are used to command. We can rail too; the difference is, women expect to be listened to." She gave him a look of astonishment, and he laughed again. "Yes you do; but we learn as little boys not to expect it. Not to argue, not to make a fuss. The world is not going to change for us. Putting up with things is our first lesson." She was not sure how serious he was, but his words grieved her, and he saw it. "Ah, Rahiké . . . Take no notice." He drew her down, whispering, "The Dreamer is wise, and all things are well. How could I wish my life different? If I were not what I am, you might not love me."

III

Summer burned to its end, and the bright colors of
the valley dulled to a dusty ripeness. Throughout
Naramethé, City and Town, all other work gave way
before the demands of Harvest. The Lodges were silent,
the Market deserted, the temples and shrines were left to
their Deities: in the quiet City even the Children's Court
was empty, for all were with their mothers in the fields.

It was the bridge between seasons; the days were hot,
but the uncertain weather of autumn was near. Any night
might bring storms, or worse, one of the tearing winds
from the mountains. Every loaded cart and filled barn was
triumph, every uncut field a whip cracking over their
heads. This work Rahiké did not command, it was too
important to be left in the hands of one so new to
authority; the Old Mistress did not keep her chair at
Harvest, and her successor dwindled to a pupil indeed.
Piety demanded that every daughter share the first day of
work on her mother's farm, although in fact Rahiké's
mother hardly needed her help, since she grew less grain
than green crops, which had a longer gathering season; but
after that the Young Mistress's concern was with the public
farmlands, and most of her time was spent going about
them. The working days were long, under a sun that
burned even the city women who were pale most of the

year; but the urgency of the task gave it zest, and there was gaiety in the shared labor. A Harvest when all went well, as it did that year, was like a long festival. It was a time Rahiké had enjoyed all her life, through all the years she had spent it on her mother's farm; but that year, riding about her beloved land with a greater harvest to gather and a greater part to play, she felt her life brimming over.

This was the only time men and women worked alongside each other. Mairilek sometimes came to the public fields, but his mother's spice garden had the first claim on him, so Rahiké rarely saw him outdoors. In what concerned the spices even more than what concerned the corn she was only a messenger, or a listener to discussions between the Mistress and the gardeners; and Mairilek's mother was a senior gardener, the overseer of one of Naramethé's largest spice gardens.

However, she saw him every night. Though they worked as long as the sun shone and were often too tired for love, they still sought each other's arms for sleep. His tan had grown rich and dark. At the sight of his black hair falling about his brown shoulders she told him he looked like a bay pony, but at the end of each day he would laugh at her skewbald body, patched with ten depths of brown where different garments had covered her, and compare her to the spatchcocked cattle. He complained that it would take him weeks after Harvest to make up the practice time he was losing, but even that could not spoil the sense of holiday. They enjoyed unaccustomed privacy too, since Burdal spent the whole of Harvest with her grandmother. On the two days that Rahiké, released from other duties, went to work on the farm, her daughter was torn between joy at seeing her and anxiety that she should understand that she couldn't talk now—she was *very busy*. Like many of the women who worked much with their minds and little with their hands, Rahiké enjoyed a limited spell of physical work in the open air; although she was ashamed to find how she fell short of her mother and sisters in strength. They were hardened to the work, but at the end of a day her hands were aching and blistered, her sides stretched, her back preparing to be stiff.

"I'm not much more use than when I was Siké's age," she said to Mairilek, "and she's nimbler than I am. It was a relief to find that I can still keep ahead of my great-aunt. *She* teases me worse than any of them; gives me her worst insult, says I'm no more use than a man." Mairilek protested, and she laughed. "No endurance, she means; I couldn't keep up the work for days at a stretch; and she's right. She takes charge of the storage now, and she always says, 'Men may bring in the first ten baskets, but the women bring in the last twenty.' My uncles only laugh now, they've heard it so often; but it is true."

"But how much is in the last twenty?" he argued. "As much as is in the first ten? I know women are tougher; I know we aren't as healthy and we haven't your stamina, but we do have muscle. I'm sure over a day the work is equal."

"And over a week?" But she was too sleepy to argue, and smiled lovingly at him. "Well, perhaps. Lie down now. Oh, don't talk to me of stamina! I'm so tired! And don't dare go in the morning, without seeing that I've managed to stand up!"

Harvest had not ended when reaping was done, but the danger of loss was over, and the beginning of threshing was an occasion for rejoicing. On the first day of it Rahiké stood with the other women to see the men dance; there was not a woman there but gazed at Mairilek, though her brother or her lover danced beside him, and Rahiké exulted in their admiration. Threshing, at least of the public crops, was by tradition left to the men, and to the young men at that, who could swing the heaviest threshing flail. Most of them enjoyed the chance to display their strength, but Mairilek hated this work; he strapped his hands for it, but still they were bruised, so that for a while they were less supple. Rahiké was sorry for it, yet she loved to watch him at the task, delighting in the ease with which he swung the heavy flail. With his body too, she always saw his grace more clearly than his strength.

No people were ever better at making holiday than the Halilaki, and the feast that celebrated the end of Harvest was the longest and gayest of the year. All who could gathered for it: the women who tended the public lands in the south, priestesses from distant shrines, herders and miners from the hills. The festival lasted five days, but the first day was best, when thank-offerings were borne to the temple of Great Rehera, Queen of Earth, and most of Naramethé went with them, singing and dancing. Women who had borne children that year led the way, carrying their babies, and the Mistress came behind them, but no other part of the procession had customary form. People went as they pleased, walking or dancing, talking, laughing, changing places. It was a day for plumes and streamers, for the rattles and cymbals that were almost all they knew of music, for anything that flashed or waved or made a noise: children darted everywhere, boys and girls and young men made acrobatic display of youth and high spirits. The great offering wains surged forward amid the happy uproar, splendidly decked and drawn by caparisoned oxen. Their decorations were traditional, but there were more fantastically ornamented carts and wagons in the crowd, some ridden on, others there for their gaiety. The men were bright as cock birds, curled and adorned, the young ones crowned with flowers or leaves. They wore kilts of an old style, draped and fringed, and the carnival clothes of the women were the antique costume of Halilak, small bodices and long full skirts. It was all merry, disorderly, magnificent; a celebration of summer, a defiance of winter, and most of all an outburst of the exuberance that is the true spirit of Halilak, now as then.

After the offering the feasting began, and they rejoiced into the night, dancing until the valley was filled with Voiha's light. It was not a time when lovers could engross each other; Mairilek, brilliant in scarlet kilt and crowned with red vine leaves, was hardly at Rahiké's side, yet she was too happy to be jealous, even when Mirrik pulled him into the dance. But when it grew late she caught his hands and they ran together from the other dancers, while she said, laughing, "Come, let's pretend we're seventeen again, with nowhere to go." He came, protesting that she must have forgotten what it was like to be seventeen, forgotten how many twigs and stones there were in the softest grass, forgotten how cold and damp midnight could be, "and if you find a good place everybody wants it"; but still he followed; though before long she agreed that there was much to be said for being older, and having a bed to go to.

Harvest was always a race against autumn, and the loser came hard behind. More and more often the wind blew from the east, wet and boisterous, and the birds fled before it. Leaves drifted in corners and house porches, insects seemed more numerous. The moist air of morning and evening drew such smells from the warm earth that unleashed dogs did not know where to run first. Mud lay in the middle of gateways and the hollows of paths. Mist dimmed the horizon and thickened the light in the woods. Yet there were spells of calm warm weather, days hot as summer, though the smells and colors of the valley had changed and the shadows did not fall as they had; then the trees glowed richly under a sun of deeper gold.

Rahiké was one who loved autumn, and the beauty made more brilliant by the poignancy of imminent loss; on the evening of such a day she sat on her stair, watching the sun paint the eastern hillsides. It was still warm, though the front of the house was in shadow, but she had already lit a fire against the later chill. She had been smoking her pipe, but now it lay beside Mairilek's unlit one, and she smelled the scents drawn up from the hollow of the valley. Behind her on the top step Burdal and Mairilek scuffled and laughed, contending to see whether he would submit to a reading lesson. It was knowledge forbidden to men, but Burdal understood that only imperfectly, and he did not spoil the game with such facts, preferring to plead laziness, stupidity, aversion. The child had hardly begun herself to master the syllabic alphabet, but every evening she would advance on him, clutching her character tiles, her eyes starting with excitement, while he cringed away and refused to look. She was growing a little too noisy; Rahiké waited for the nudge of his foot and then turned, as if she had only just heard and been shocked. "Burdal! Are you telling Mairilek secrets?"

The little girl hopped back, looking from one to the other, giggling. She was never sure how real this rebuke was. "All right," she said, suddenly docile, and put the tiles on the bench; then she cried, "I'm going to play on your box, Uncle Mairilek!"

He sprang to his feet and caught it out of her way. "No. Not tonight. Tonight it is dedicated." She capered before him arguing, but he sat down, clasping the instrument to him. "No." His face was grave. Rahiké stood up, but Burdal was already sobering. She sighed. "All right," she said again; then, "I think I'll go to bed now."

He was sitting on the steps again when Rahiké returned, the music box leaning on the wall behind him. She sat on the step below and leaned against his knee. In a while he tugged her headcloth lightly, and she caught at it. "No, don't, I'll wear it out here. It gives them one thing less to say."

"I only wanted to make you speak. Why are you so quiet?"

"Oh, thinking. About the money." She and the Mistress were trying to fix a better rate at which the clay tallies on the public foodstores that were their usual currency could be exchanged for the metal money needed to trade outside Naramethé. "I was wondering—how did you get the trade-money for your box? Surely you don't make bets in metal? Yet the changers would have been surprised—I wouldn't have thought they would do it for you."

"No, I didn't think it either. I didn't try; Master Dairek changed it for me."

"Did he know what you meant to do with it?"

"He didn't ask."

After a moment she said, "He is very fond of you, isn't he?"

"He is a kind Master to us all. But yes, I think so. He was when I was a child. He was my mother's lover for a long time."

"Does that make a difference?" she said blandly.

"Well, of course. Would a son of yours be only another child to me?" She looked up at him, but his face was innocent. "Is Burdal? What you love, I love."

He wore a wreath of the year's last golden flowers, and in his tanned face his eyes glowed more brilliant than ever. Suddenly Rahiké felt enormously happy. She leaned her arms on his knees and smiled rapturously at him. "You are so beautiful!" she marveled. "You even have a beautiful nose. Plain men often have fine eyes, and good mouths are not so rare, but a beautiful nose—!" He smiled tranquilly; compliments neither confused nor elated him; he accepted them with sedate pleasure. "I shall have to mar you somehow before the frosts come; break your nose? What do you think? Or Nehaté will forget Hiramarrek, and cast her love on you."

His face quivered slightly, "Poor Hiramarrek."

She laughed. "Would you run from her? Or is a Goddess's kiss worth dying for?"

He answered without her lightness. "If I fled would you come too? Or I might as well stay and die." He took her hands and looked at her so earnestly he almost seemed sorrowful. "Rahiké; would you love me if I were not beautiful?"

She raised her brows and laughed again. "Oh! Is this the modesty for which you are praised?"

"Should I believe you lie, then?" He shook his head, and tightened his grasp of her hands. "Don't laugh at me, Rahiké. Karathek shaped me well, and I am grateful; Dairek would not thank his pots for dispraising themselves. But my mirror says to me, 'This will not last, what else have you?'" She had rarely known him so intense, and her levity faded. He said, "I am glad if my face pleases you; but there is sickness, accident, age—I may not always be beautiful. Will you always love me?"

She answered with passion. "Of course I will! Oh, Mairilek, how can you doubt it? It is not your face I love!" Yet it was not so easy to answer his question. If he had not been so lovely, would he have been the same person? The knowledge of that beauty, the consequences of it, had helped to shape him. "Not now. But if you had not been as you are, or if it had not been for your music, I might not have noticed you: that is true. No, but I saw you were beautiful from the beginning; I did not love you so soon."

In a moment he said in his ordinary voice, "Now you have crushed me. I loved you much sooner than that. As soon as you said, 'They play in the presence of the Queen,' I began to love you."

She laughed faintly. "What a lot of time I wasted! No, not wasted. If you eat the grape you can't drink the wine."

Soon after he asked, "Is it your birthday soon?"

"Yes, in four days. Why?"

He did not answer her directly, but picked up his pipe. "Listen; do you remember this?" He played a quick flicker of music, and she smiled.

"Is it the way I laugh?"

He nodded, looking pleased. "There are others too; the way you talk sometimes"—he made more shapes of sound—"see, I can hear you speak even when I am away. But the laugh is most important. That is what I used most."

"Used?"

He put the pipe aside and reached for his music box, while she watched, perplexed. "Sit over there," he said. "I need a little more room."

She moved, increasingly surprised. "I thought you said the music box was dedicated."

"It is: to this." He began testing the strings. "Other men take their lovers gifts on their birthday that they have made; and I didn't think you would like my pottery. So I made you this." He gave her a fleeting glance; not for months had she seen him shy and uncertain. "Listen," he said, and began to play.

It was the longest music he had ever made, and past measure the loveliest. Rahiké listened—at first with astonished pleasure; until wonder became awe, and awe dread. Presently she turned away from the sight of his agile cunning fingers, his exalted face, and rested her eyes blindly on the hills.

She had not understood. In Naramethé they knew no music but song, and that which marked the beat for dancing; and though she had learned better than that, Rahiké had still no more than a vague sense of what else it might be. Now she recalled in bitter shame how she had talked to him of "tunes," and how in all he did she had heard the absent voices, or imagined the dance. All these months she had listened to him, had been proud of being wiser than her sisters, had presumed to think herself a sharer in his mystery; and all that she had learned had brought her no nearer understanding than this. She had come far in darkness, but now light broke and showed her the unimagined length of the road she could never travel, how far beyond her reach were the distant paths where he walked; and she was overwhelmed by grief and fear.

Music was this: it needed no words, it spoke of itself, pure, self-sufficient, remote; it was she who was isolated by it now. At last she comprehended its power and divinity, but the face of this Immortal was veiled from her. In a terrified vision she saw Mairilek as one of the heroes to whom the craftsmen made offerings, seated before the shadowy feet of the austere and complex Deity he made manifest. And all the time, the intricate beauty he had created for her, Rahiké, spilled from his hands like water from a spring. She yearned to drink of that water, but as she tried it turned to mist and drifted away. Though she listened with desperate attention as the melodies swelled and curved about her, flowed together, mingled, parted, there was nothing she could hold. She thought she heard the laugh-shape sometimes, but oddly changed, and if she learned to recognize a group of sounds they seemed to reappear altered, as if painted in a different color. All she understood was that it was beautiful, and alien to her mind. Yet he had made this glory for her, to speak to her; he was telling her he loved her, eloquently, intensely, but in a foreign tongue. It was the greatest gift he could offer her: and she could not receive it.

When silence fell, she could not break it. She wanted to weep, to take him in her arms, to pull him back from the far strange places. It was he who spoke first, saying diffidently, "Well, there were not too many mistakes." She drew her eyes back from the hills and turned them on him, though what he might see in them she dared not guess. He was looking at her anxiously. He awaited her acceptance, her approval, and the thought of his skill imploring blessing of her ignorance moved her beyond gladness or pain. At last the joy came, swelling her heart. What matter if he did go beyond her reach? He would always come back to her. He loved her.

"Oh, such a gift!" she whispered; "I never deserved such a gift." She was not sure herself what she meant, but his eyes brightened. They grew hopeful; but what could she say, how could she speak over such a distance? What words could she find that would not reveal her incapacity? Those that lay nearest her tongue were useless. If she spoke of how difficult it must have been, or asked how long it had taken him, or how he remembered it all, she knew she would see his face fade into disappointment. He wanted praise for his creation, not his diligence, and praising pottery adequately had been beyond her.

"I do not know what to say," she confessed huskily. "I never thought you could make anything so beautiful. I would only insult it if I tried to praise it. I do not know the words, Mairilek. Shall I use words made to speak of—of color—of eating—of things to see and touch? I need a new language to speak about this. I do not know the words."

Yet it was not enough, and she cried passionately, "Only Voiha knows them! Oh, no wonder this is called a Power! This is not a craft; it is more than that, it is something new; if there is a name for it I do not know what it is! To make out of nothing, nothing at all— It is more, much more, than I ever knew! It is part of Voiha's dreaming!"

So it was he who took her in his arms, and she wept after all, though very briefly. "I hoped you would like it," he said; and then they both laughed feebly. He said, "It is the way I can tell you what I feel. Words can speak my mind, but only this speaks my heart." She thought, And when your heart speaks I am deaf; and she hid her face in his hair.

After a while she drew back and said in her normal voice, "Now I shall ask the stupid questions. When did you do this? It was not made in an evening, but I never heard it before."

"You have, small pieces of it. They don't sound the same when I practice them alone. I have been making it a long time. I began after that first evening I came to play, and you offered me the porch. I didn't know then what it would be, of course. I only knew that, that—" His voice stumbled. "I knew I wanted to put you—to make you into music. When I could not be with you, it would comfort me, that I could play you. And the more I knew you, the richer the music grew. Then, about a month ago—no, more, there was Harvest—I saw how I could make it well, most of it, into this."

"And I asked you for tunes!" she mourned. But he laughed.

"Well, you were right. Tunes were what I was making, most of the time. I didn't know how to go beyond them. It took me a long time to find this."

"You said you 'used' the laugh sound. What did you mean?"

He struggled to explain, but in the end could only shrug and look exasperated. She had understood nothing. She smiled and touched his lips. "I told you so; only Voiha knows the words. Oh, Mairilek! This is one of the Holy Ones, I know it is! They have chosen you to bring something new into the world!"

But her words frightened them both. "Hush!" he said, holding her tighter, and she turned the talk another way. "You have learned so much since the spring, more than I guessed. What has made the difference? The box? Or having a place to work?"

"Both. And more than that. It is having someone who listens."

She was silenced. He bent and kissed her, and said fervently, "Life is too short for me to be grateful enough. If I have music, Rahiké, it is because you have given it to me."

She pushed her fingers into his hair. "If that is so, then it is the midwife and not Rehera who gives children."

"Well," he replied seriously, "and is it not sometimes the midwife who defeats Nité when she would lock up the womb?"

Rahiké began to laugh weakly. "Oh, my love, where did you learn to say such things? Is this what comes of one boy in a family of girls? We must watch our Sinak carefully, then. I don't want a blasphemous brother!" She stood up and tugged at his hand. "It's getting cold now; come inside. I want to hear my music again."

Whether Voiha dreamed them so, or whether the life of Halilak made them so, it was true that few men looked beyond the immediate future. Mairilek was not one of them. It was Rahiké who began to think anxiously of the years to come. Now that she had begun to understand the magnitude and strangeness of his gift she wondered how much still lay beyond her comprehension, and how Naramethé was to accommodate such a thing. She had respected what he did from the first, moved by his dedication, but when she believed a new God was speaking, she grew afraid. How could Naramethé receive a new God

and not be changed? If it would not change, what would
become of the Deity's servants? What would become of
Naramethé? The Holy Ones could not be rejected, and
they were a strong sisterhood. Goddesses when they
chose to reveal themselves must be honored, or all
Heaven was insulted.

Rahiké loved and valued stability, and abhorred anything that threatened it; the revulsion was learned so
young by women of her race, and buried so deep in them,
that it was almost an instinct. They hated change. In those
days she remembered a terrible thing that had happened in
the Town when she was a child. Two men had fought: not
the childish scuffling that little boys were shamed out of,
not the quick blow derided and punished in older youths,
but a real fight, that had brought the Town to a shocked
halt and left both men injured. Like wild dogs, said all
who had seen it. For a year afterwards both men had
dragged burdens like beasts, their criminal hands locked
into wooden yokes, and children had screamed and fled
from the sight of them. But little Rahiké had lived for
weeks in a terror that caused her to hide from the burly
uncles whose strength she had loved until then; fearing
that a law once broken was destroyed, its protection gone.
Now that fear came back to her, and the understanding
that those men had broken something even more precious
than law; they had broken custom.

And so had she. She felt herself two people, one
rebuking the other. That she, the Young Mistress, should
have done this! She, who should know better than any that
law and custom were not to be defied, that they were the
mortar of society and its safeguard against disintegration.
Not respecting the Town, she had not sufficiently respected
its laws. It had seemed nothing terrible to bring him the
music box, to offer him a place to practice; nothing of the
men's world was a serious matter. She had tossed a stone
carelessly, and now behind her heard the rumble of the
avalanche.

This was not a game, a pastime he could pursue

between making pots. It seemed her mother had been right after all, and Mekiné, and the Town. The only safe thing to do with such a gift as his was to crush it, as she plucked tree seedlings from the paving of her courtyard lest they grow and lift the stones she walked on. Yet she could not believe it; could not have done it. Though she dreaded change as her sisters did, though his music did not speak to her, though as most Halilaki would be she was baffled by its lack of purpose, she could not regret what she had done, and not only because she loved him. It was because she feared impiety even more than change. Rahiké was no more of a mystic than other women, yet she could not lose the sense of a great presence behind him. The Immortals could not be denied.

It was often said that men worshipped the Goddesses, women served them; indeed, men joked that the women's first concern was to strike a bargain with them, and there was truth in that. Once Rahiké had comprehended the importance of his music she immediately sought to learn its implications, how it would affect his life, how it might stretch beyond him: what demands the new Deity made, what compromise it might accept, and what needed to be done. Mairilek's response was simpler. Like most men, he found a blind faith in the Holy Ones quite natural; they had all been brought up not to question, to obey without understanding, to know the world was in wiser hands than theirs. Rahiké's apprehensions did not touch her lover, and when she talked of the future he was unconcerned. For the present the lonely struggle to increase his skill sufficed him. He had come farther along his road than he had once thought possible; only a little time ago he had not dreamed of being so fortunate. His knowledge, his assurance, his craftsmanship grew. He had not yet reached a point where he could learn no more of himself, nor begun to hunger for the companionship of his peers. Rahiké's praise satisfied him still; in those days he had not learned his need for discerning criticism. Rahiké, faithful to her nature and her training, sought a context for his music, but he, a true craftsman, saw nothing but his given task and cared only to do it well. Also, he loved Rahiké. The present seemed perfect to him, and he had no temptation to look beyond it.

It never ceased to grieve Rahiké that music remained meaningless to her, of value only because he made it. Though she listened diligently anything more complex than the melody of a song was beyond her grasp; and all he did grew more and more complex. It was lovely and impenetrable; it put the frost in her heart. She could not have borne that he should know it to be so, and had to take care than an inept remark did not betray her, so she dared to speak less and less. It would have delighted her to be able to praise his work intelligently, instead of fearing that her commendation, if he heeded it, could only mislead him. She knew that if she liked one thing better than another it meant only that it was simpler to follow; that she did not have an ear that could tell good music from bad any more than she had Nehsa's eye for what was good in a pony; but she came to fear that her preference was for the worst, and that what she liked in the work the craftsman would have despised.

It was so not only with the music but with the way he played it. False notes passed her by, and so long as the music did not stop she did not know whether he played well or ill; nor did she realize that the manner of his playing mattered. Once when she was listening, particularly impressed by his skill, he stopped, sweeping a hand across the strings, and said in disgust, "A Master would not let me get away with that."

"Why not?" she asked, immeasurably relieved that she had not spoken her admiration.

"Showy. Shallow. Like using spices until you can't taste the meat. Like decorating a cup until no one could drink from it. I was saying, 'Listen to me being clever!'"

To deceive the ignorant, she thought. "And you should have been saying, 'Listen to the music'?"

"Yes, I should. Which may mean that I don't really

believe that this music is worth listening to." He looked displeased. "Or it could just mean that I was being lazy."

"It sounded difficult," she said tentatively; but he replied irritably, "It isn't meant to *sound* difficult."

The knowledge that others did not share her dullness of ear did not make it easier to bear. One evening late in autumn she went down to unleash the porch dog, and was startled to find her mother standing at the foot of the stairs. Rahiké exclaimed, and began to greet her, but she was hurriedly gestured into silence. She obeyed, surprised. They stood together in the shadows, listening to Mairilek's playing. It was something new: hard, austere music that had driven Rahiké from the room. Now she watched her mother's face in amazement. It showed strained attention, more bewilderment than pleasure, but the music was not mere sound to her; she was inside that glittering curtain. Her daughter grew sad and envious, and walked away to fetch the dog. The music checked as Mairilek began to work on one group of notes. Rahiké released the leash, and the sound was obscured by claws scrambling on the stairs and porch. Her mother turned to her and said, "Is that your boy?"

"Yes, of course. Why are you standing here? Why not come up?"

"I didn't want to disturb him." She held out a child's cape. "Burdal left this, and I thought she might need it before she came again; and I thought, it's a nice night, I'll walk down. But when I got this far, I heard that." She shook her head. "I didn't come up because I thought he might stop." Rahiké looked at her in silence, thinking that this was a strange way for jealousy to come to her. Her mother looked subdued and disturbed. "That isn't like anything I ever heard before. I never thought of it being like that. Songs and dances were what I thought, nothing to neglect a craft for. I thought a face was all he had."

Rahiké smiled. "Well, he has that too. Come up and see. And hear; there's much more to hear."

"No, no, I might spoil it. He might not like to play with me there."

"He'll be glad. No one but me listens to him. Mairilek will be so pleased, if you want to hear, if you like his playing."

"No, I can't; after all I've said about him!" She turned away, but Rahiké caught her arm and said gently, "You didn't know him. I want you to know him. Come in, Mother; do come in. It's not kind to walk away from your daughter's door. Come and meet Mairilek. Indeed, Mother, it's time you did."

Winter began. Mairilek helped her fit the panels between the porch rails, and the slatted shutters that closed the upper part, so that the wind's force was broken before it reached the house windows. The long room grew dark, especially after they fetched the porch door out of the storeroom and hung it at the top of the stairs. They lived by lamplight and firelight. Out of doors Rahiké bound her trousers at the ankle and wore a quilted coat, regretting yet again that by custom women did not wear wool; but despite their warmth Mairilek hated his winter clothes. Under the heavy circular cloak he wore his summer kilts and went barelegged and bare chested as long as he could endure to do so. Rahiké was amused. "Who is it you want to impress? Nehaté, maybe? If she meets you dressed like that you won't be able to resist her." He was so cold she recoiled from touching him. "Anyway, you're better looking when you're warm." At last he put on a tunic and a longer, thicker kilt, but it took the frosts to make him wear stockings and breeches. Rahiké had never seen him look so sulky as on the evening he first appeared in all his detested garments. Certainly they did not become him as well as the near nakedness of summer, but when she teased him for his vanity he grumbled, "It isn't that. They itch, and they tickle. And you would not laugh if you had to wash them. That's what 'winter' means to me: the Lodge reeking of damp wool."

He came to the house earlier now, since work in the Lodges ended with daylight. Burdal was rapturous that he so often arrived before she was in bed; it made each day seem privileged. She declared fervently that winter was the best time of year, and if the lovers could not quite agree, they both enjoyed the season that year as never before. Mairilek relished the longer darkness which freed him for his music; Rahiké delighted in the tranquil firelit evenings when work was done and the lamps dimmed, when he played and she watched him, or gazed into the flames and told herself that she must never forget to know how happy she was, that not a moment must pass unnoticed. For happiness cannot be held perfect for ever: if fortune does not mar it staleness will, since mortals grow weary of anything.

Sometimes they leaned together before the hearth, talking, or they piled cushions before it and lay together in the pool of warmth; sometimes the cold seemed to eat the fire, and nowhere was warm but bed. Yet Rahiké found it was possible to love winter for more than its long nights, not only for what it gave but what it was. She had never looked before at the beauty of stars on a night of frost, or of the moons swollen and soft in cloudy air; had never noticed the tinsel trimming of hoarfrost glorifying a dead leaf, nor how bright the leafless woods could be under the pale sun. No loveliness less than new snow had reached her, and even so she could not remember ever having seen streams running blue in the shadow of their white banks, the fragile peaks of the snow balanced on leaves and twigs, the continual faint glitter in the air as it sifted from its perches to the ground. She gazed now in wonder, amazed to think that the world had always been so. There had always been this profound stillness, this weight of cloud, these quiet animals huddled together in the mist of their breathing. Naked trees had lifted their delicate

tracery against white skies every winter of her life, and
she had never seen it. Now she found pleasure even in the
bleakness of the ploughed fields, in the unyielding frost in
the earth and the dank smells of milder days, for they all
held the peace of the fallow season. It was more than a
quickened awareness: Rahiké had become part of the
world. The joy Mairilek had brought her reached beyond
him, and she lived now in her heart's excess. Once winter
had been like night, a gap in time, but there were no
more gaps in her life. Not even when they were apart.
She missed him, yet his absence was not now a breach in
living. She had learned to believe in happiness.

It was as well that separation had become endurable.
A dry winter could be a good time for journeys if they
were not long, the roads being easier in frost than in mud,
and that season Rahiké traveled several times to neighbor-
ing lands. It was her business to know these places and
their rulers, and to be known by them. She enjoyed the
duty, and the sense that her name had weight outside
Naramethé. However, she was startled to find that in
temple-ruled Varaskil they had heard of her lover too.
That was a place famous for its sheep, and she was buying
for him two tunics of bleached wool, so fine that they
could not be unpleasant to wear, when the woman accom-
panying her observed that white was the proper clothing
for beauty and inquired by name after the lovely Mairilek.
Priestesses had a reputation for knowing everything and
liked to sustain it, but few men had names that crossed
borders, and she had not expected his to be known.

She was gone eight days on that journey; her longest
absence. Custom could never harden her to leaving her
child, and the first evening of her return always belonged
to Burdal. Mairilek did not come until very late, when the
child had fallen asleep; though after so long apart, neither
wanted greetings decorous enough for Burdal's presence.
Such homecomings were almost worth the absence; but
not quite. Pain that could be borne was still pain.

He was delighted with his gift; white garments were a

luxury, and Rahiké was pleased to see how well they became him. The news of his fame amused him, though he was quick to point out that it was hers, not his own. "It is not like being a great craftsman known from here to Halkal-Mari."

"Are there many such?" she asked, for she had never heard of a foreign Master.

"No, not many, or there would be no honor in it."

"Nor are many men known as you are. Would you rather be heard of in the Towns than in the Cities?"

"Known for what I did, and not for what the God had done? Of course I would!"

The notion that he might wish for fame was new and touching; such acclaim was so far beyond the reach of one who would never be a Master that it would have saddened her if it had seemed to sadden him. However, his spirits were so high she could not grieve for him, nor believe ambition was any stronger in him than in his sister. All boys were taught to hope for glory as craftsmen; it was no more than that, no dream of his own.

The day after her return from Varaskil he said, "Rahiké, come and listen; I have something for you to hear." It was always so when she returned from a journey; this time he was very animated, and rather unsure.

"Sit down; it will take a little while. I don't know if I can do it. I had an idea, but I don't know if I've found the way to make it work. I keep practicing, but I can't always get it right."

She sat down, intrigued by this uncertainty. He kept putting his pipe to his lips with one hand, then taking it away while he arranged the fingers of the other hand on the music box. At last he began, frowning with concentration, playing the strings and the pipe together. But they did not play the same note, nor, so far as Rahiké could tell, the same tune. The sound was strange and halting; she was bewildered. Soon Mairilek took the pipe away with a shake of his head. "I lost it. I'll try again." This time he faltered less, but to Rahiké it was still only a tangle of sound. Prevarication was impossible, and alarm made her abrupt; as soon as he stopped she said, "I'm sorry, I didn't understand at all."

He laughed wryly, looking at the two instruments. "I'm not surprised. No one could understand that jumble. I hardly played two right notes together, and I muddled the time. Nothing was right. It was nothing like it at all."

"Like what?"

"Like the sound I want. The sound I *hear*." He rubbed his head. "Playing them both at once is even harder than I thought it would be. I get muddled. And I can't play the sort of music I want, as I first thought it. I have to make something that only needs one hand for each."

"You thought first of each tune needing two? Two hands on each instrument? But—that would need two musicians to play it."

He looked up, smiling, rueful. "Yes, it would. I suppose that makes it seem a waste of time, but I had to try it, once I had thought of it. Maybe I can't ever play it, but I must know how it could be done. I'll try again. Listen."

He played a short tune on the music box, then one on the pipe. "I want to put those together. Like weaving with two colors." He looked at her, then pushed the instruments aside. "It's no use, I can't explain. I can hear it in my head, but I can't show you."

"But you weren't playing the same tune!"

"No; that's the point of it. There would be nothing special in just playing one tune twice."

"But it makes a muddle!"

"Only because I'm not doing it right."

"How can they fit together if they're not the same tune? They can't!"

"I think they can." He knelt before her and took her hands. "I want to find out *how* they can." He looked at her, perturbed, and stroked her cheek. "What's the matter?"

"I wish I could understand!"

"I wish I could explain. It's my fault. Think of weaving, as I said; different colors. Or cooking with spices. Blending things. Think of something made from wood and metal; two qualities for one purpose." He searched her eyes, and his voice changed. "Oh, Rahiké! Never mind all that. Think of making love. We are not doing the same things; yet we are doing one thing, doing it together, something we could never do alone."

Rahiké loosed her hands and put her arms around him. He whispered, "Things don't have to be the same to belong together. Being different—we are different, very different, but we belong together. Don't we? Say we do. Kiss me."

He never had to beg. Now in the recoil from fear and jealousy she had to strive to curb a passion that seemed to her to be desperate and ridiculous. Presently he muttered, "Everything I learn comes from you, everything I know. I can't say how much I love you."

"Mairilek; Mairilek! You should have explained like this at first. I think I begin to understand." She laughed shakily. "I didn't know tunes could make love!"

He raised his head smiling. "Not all of them can—or will. I can't tell you why, I don't know." He loosened his arms and went back to the bench, picking up his music box and stroking his nails up the strings. "These are the times I need a Master."

How short-lived relief could be. The words sank through her and lay cold in her belly. She said foolishly, "To play with you?"

"No—oh, yes—no, to help me. Rahiké, that comes to me like something really new. But how do I know? Perhaps a Master could tell me if there are rules—how many tunes I can use, the sort, the—oh, I don't know! But every craft has its rules. This, these two tunes; I think it would work; but how can I know if I can never play them?" He began plucking the strings softly. "But it's a waste of time talking about it. There are no other musicians in Naramethé."

He sounded calm enough, even cheerful; Rahiké

could not believe he was repining. Yet it was hard for her to understand how he could say such things so blithely. When he had spoken of needing other musicians she had seen the air grow thick with shadows and heard night scratch at the doors of her heart. Now as the dread receded she chided herself again. If he did need comrades, even if by a miracle he could have them, would it make his love for her less? Was he, only because he was a man, to find all he needed in her? Was his life to be so confined? This was the shame of the distant northern women with their house-dwelling lovers, that they kept men like children. Such enfolding love was monstrous, despicable, and she would not yield to it.

But reason and decision could not banish the smell of grief. Until he came, her winged soul had been pinioned, no more able to fly than a farmyard goose. Now, it soared. Without him there would be nothing for her to do but to fold her wings and waddle back into her pen.

After midwinter the weather softened for a time, and the season became a matter of rain and mud. The puddles in Mekiné's courtyard were deep and reached out to each other; Rahiké had to pick a way between them, and with her eyes on the ground she did not at first notice the woman seated on the porch. The High Priestess of Rehera was there, a tall middle-aged woman, becoming heavy but still floridly handsome. Rahiké was surprised, knowing there was no liking between her and Mekiné. The Lady Beharé served her Goddess honestly, and robed and in her temple she was high and majestic; but though at all times a proud, commanding woman, she seemed to put off her greatness with her robes. Rahiké had no great regard for her, but the Priestess could not be ignored, and she was astute and practical as well as influential. The Young Mistress had learned to feel only civil indifference toward women she had to work with but could not like, and would have talked without reluctance; however, her companion seemed unwilling, for once, to do so. After saying something about speaking to Mekiné concerning some incense, she folded her arms and stared into the rain. Rahiké was surprised and rather offended, then after a while amused at their situation; a spice garden in winter offered little pretext for the close attention they were both giving it. The ground where the bushes grew was walled in and roofed over now, and where the shutters were open they were canopied to keep out rain. The only things to watch were the smoke from the stove chimney—thin today, for it was not cold—and the merging rings on the puddles.

It was not long before Mekiné and a young priestess emerged to interrupt their silence. The Lady Beharé stood up, seeming no more eager to talk to Mekiné, beyond asking whether her requirements had been met; and Rahiké wondered why she had given herself the trouble of the walk when her subordinate could have done the work as well. Mekiné only smiled a greeting to her, but the young priestess, one of Mirrik's friends, grinned at her and said, "Hello, and how is the woman with the prettiest pillow in Halilak?"

Rahiké retorted gaily, "I don't know; who is she?"; but the High Priestess gave an angry exclamation and broke in. "You've spoiled that boy, Rahiké!"

Rahiké paused and stared at the High Priestess, astonished. There was no mistaking her temper. The Young Mistress saw the hostility in her eyes, and her own grew stern.

"How have I done so?" she said, though her forbidding tone did not invite criticism. The Priestess's mouth grew small, and she hitched at her heavy mantle.

"There used to be no sweeter boy in Naramethé."

Such descriptions of her lover always irritated Rahiké. "But he grew up, is that what you mean? That happened before I knew him, and I could not have prevented it."

"Grew up? What has that to do with it? I am saying he has lost his manners!" Her voice had swollen to the tones she used to fill her temple. "He is conceited, insolent; he has no respect! Being the favorite of the Young Mistress has turned his head! His conduct would be unbecoming in a Master."

Her acolyte turned circumspectly away; Mekiné looked down with a smile. Rahiké said calmly, "I have seen nothing of that, nor heard it from anyone else. If you mean he is more confident than he used to be, I hope he is; and if you mean he suffers insults less meekly, I am glad to hear it." She would have said more, had she not been so amazed by Beharé's reaction. Whatever the cause of her anger, these words heated rather than cooled it. Her high color shrank into patches; she drew her ringed hands up under her breasts, and her jaw thickened.

"Is it likely many people would say such things to you?" Her top lip lifted; but when she met Rahiké's hard, golden stare she seemed to lose hold of her next words, and said only, "Aaaah, Queen of Earth. . . . Why should I think you would listen to reason about him? Such bedfellows are forgiven everything. But you've spoiled him for all that, and one day you'll suffer for it!"

She stepped down from the porch with a swing of her heavy skirts and strode off, pulling the mantle over her head. The young priestess grimaced and followed. Mekiné watched their departure with delight; it was not easy to be haughty when hopping between puddles. "Well!" said Rahiké. "Do you understand that?"

"Yes, I do. Raha, you were so near; I thought she was going to spit on you!"

"She would have raised a blister; a bite would have killed me. 'Such bedfellows,' gah! But why? Has Mairilek been rude to her? I can't believe it."

Mekiné sniffed scornfully. "Not as rude as she deserved. But come in and get dry; I'll make us a drink."

Rahiké followed her saying, "But it isn't like him. And she is Rehera's Priestess, Meké; he should show her respect."

"Oh, should he? I was thoroughly pleased with him,

and I wouldn't be surprised if Queen Rehera felt the same!" Rahiké sat down; the children peered round their door and smiled at her, then vanished again. Mekiné went on talking from the kitchen. "What he does to annoy her is only what he's been doing for eight or nine years. You wouldn't want him to stop now."

"Oh, so that's it!"

"Why do you think she was here today? Only because she knows it is a holiday for the Potters—she knows everything about the Town—and she thought he might be here. It isn't for the pleasure of seeing me. But that isn't all of it. You'll have to drink green-leaf, I haven't any dark left; it wasn't very good anyway. No, even *she* could hardly call that insolent and conceited. This happened while you were in Varaskil. She was lucky that time; he was here when she called. Mairilek would have gone out when she came—and that's good enough manners—but first she insisted he stay, then she settled down to turn it into a visit. Well, you know the way she talks."

"She is coarse, I suppose. But so is the Mistress."

"Oh, Raha, they are nothing like! The Old Mistress is never nasty, but that one—she makes the walls sweat. She has a gross, mean soul. And she is worse with the young ones. It surprises me that she still ogles Mairilek, at his age. Tirek tells me that he would never send an apprentice on an errand to her, not even if he had to go himself instead."

"Really?" said Rahiké with interest. Mekiné came in and began setting a small table.

"Well, yes, but I shouldn't— Anyway, that day, everything she said may have been said *to me* but it was said *at him*. What she gets out of it I don't know, unless she just enjoys embarrassing them. But he wasn't embarrassed. I was getting really angry and thinking, High Priestess or not, I have to throw her out, when Mairilek stood up." Mekiné giggled, a sound her friend had not heard for years. Rahiké said appreciatively, "What did he say?"

"Not much; I hardly noticed, I was so surprised;

something about women's conversation being over his head, he would not intrude longer—it was not what he said. It was the way he *looked* at her. As if—I don't know—as if he'd put her down a lot faster than he'd pick her up; but that's weak. You should have seen the shock on her face. You can't imagine the way he looked at her!"

Rahiké shuddered and laughed. "I can, you know. But he was civil? Well, good! Let her try her games in my house; there's a good flight of steps from my porch." She snapped her fingers at one of the dogs, who came up to have his neck rubbed. "'No sweeter boy in Naramethé,' bah!" But she smiled to herself; not that there was, of course.

Mekiné stirred honey into the steaming cups and handed one to her, then sat back on the rug. Rahiké sipped in silence a while, brooding. She was not sorry Mairilek had snubbed the Lady Beharé, but she wished there had been no occasion for it. She was constantly trying to devise a way of giving him a better future, though knowing in her heart that such plans were hopeless. All of them would need changes in the laws of Naramethé, and she had little chance of winning consent to that; none, if she could not look for the support of the Temple of Great Rehera.

Mekiné said tentatively, "What's this I hear about Mirrik? Her friend then seemed to think she was pregnant—but—?"

"Well; yes, she thinks she may be. I didn't think she was sure enough yet to tell anyone, or I'd have said something to you. But I never heard of a priestess who could keep a secret. Perhaps it's the strain of keeping them for Goddesses." She held out her cup for refilling. "I was surprised, I must admit. Thadek won't even be three when it's born—I'd listed Mirrik among the every-five-years women. Perhaps Zoharé's baby was too much to withstand at close quarters."

"Unless it was not intended—?"

"*Mirrik?* You're joking!"

"And what about you?"

"Oh, no." She grinned, but her friend looked at her doubtfully, saying, "I don't know if Mairilek—you see, he never stayed long with anyone before."

Rahiké looked amused. "Why blame Mairilek? Look how long it took me to conceive Burdal. Years and years."

"Not so long, when you started trying."

"Well, but who says I'm trying?" Yet the thought, never before occurring, that in past years some other woman might have taken a child from Mairilek shook her with sudden rage, and her cup jarred on the table as she set it down. "Or who says which way I'm trying?"

Mekiné stared at her. "You mean you don't *want* a baby?"

"I'm sorry, I can't, not yet. Veraha forgive me—Rehera—All-Mother Maha forgive me—but I don't. Everyone thinks I must be jealous of Mirrik; but I feel like telling her to keep away, it might be catching."

"But why? Was it so hard with Burdal? You never said. Besides, she was your first."

"Name of Fire, it isn't that! No, but Burdal and I are good friends now; it's fun, the two of us, why should I want to—" She met her friend's eyes, and smiled wryly. "What lies I tell. Mekiné, don't ever, ever repeat this; not even to Mirrik; let them all think it's work that I prefer. But it's because of Mairilek."

In face of such disbelief it was hard to keep her composure. She added hurriedly, "Oh, there have been times—Zoharé's baby is trying to crawl now, and he knows me, and Burdal loves him; then, little Thadek is such fun. And once, in the snow, Mairilek was playing with Burdal—oh, of course I think sometimes I would enjoy one, but then—"

Her hands had begun to tremble; she gripped them together and leaned her brow on them. Her agitated voice stumbled. "But when Mairilek is with me, I think, how can I want anything else? What more can there be?" Mekiné eyed her in wonder. "I know it is almost sure to happen, in time. I know I will love the child when it comes; but, I don't want it now—not yet. Now, I can only think it would be something to—interfere."

After a while Mekiné said, "You never do anything the *ordinary* way, Raha." She smiled, tipping the cold dregs in her cup. "A good thing my brother can't hear this! To care more for a man than for the hope of children!"

Rahiké muttered, "Don't laugh at me. I know it's excessive. It's Karinané's revenge."

"For slighting her so long? Maybe it is. I'm not laughing. You were snowbound a long, long time. This is only a spring flood; it will pass." Mekiné rose to move the little table, and changed the subject. "Maybe Mirrik will be lucky with a girl this time."

Rahiké shook her head. "She doesn't want a girl. She says boys are best for her; she is a third daughter—she has no inheritance to leave daughters of her own. There is sense in that, I suppose, if she means to stay on the farm all her life."

"And does she?"

"It seems so." She grinned faintly; not long before she had suggested to her sister that she might consider becoming overseer of one of the public spice-gardens, and Mirrik's opinion of a life spent cosseting such delicate charges was not for Mekiné's ears. "No, wish her sons, if you would please her."

"Veraha have mercy! She will have a lonely old age!"

"She says she doesn't care for that. She'll forgo grandchildren. Mirrik is harder than you think."

Rahiké teased Mairilek when next she saw him with having offended the High Priestess, but he only said, "It is fair, then, she offended me." He looked up and smiled. "Besides, I can see that you are pleased with me."

"Of course I'm not. You should be civil. Horrible woman!"

She watched him examine the music box to see no rain had reached it. He was wearing one of his white tunics, and a heavy jerkin of dark blue. His winter clothes no longer seemed graceless; he looked solid and warm. "Poor Beharé! She used to think you were such a pleasant boy."

"No, she did not," he retorted vigorously. "She thought I was so much bone and muscle."

She laughed. "Alas, Mairilek, there are women thinking such thoughts all over Naramethé. You can't expect anything else. If you want to be admired for your soul, you'll have to get Voiha to dream you another world." Just for once, she had not been thinking of his music; but as she spoke she though of the cause he had for such wishing, and bit her mouth. He said only, "At the moment I'd be pleased enough if she'd stop dreaming of rain."

"Don't say that; if this goes on the road will be too bad for me to go to Ruthathé."

"Not another journey! Let it rain until the hills melt, then."

For a while it seemed it would do so, and if they were pleased, no one else was. Mekiné hovered more anxiously than usual about her incense bushes, which hated extreme damp as much as cold; the ailments of mild, damp winters began to be common. Floors seemed to have a permanent film of mud; children, confined indoors, grew boisterous and troublesome, and it seemed to Rahiké that all Naramethé began to grow short tempered. When her mother moaned like all farmers that this was the very worst kind of weather they could be having, and the Young Mistress replied cheerfully that she had yet to hear from a farmer of weather that was not, even Mirrik retorted with a snap that such remarks possibly seemed quite funny to people who had not been spending their day cleaning drains. Rahiké excused her sister's irritability on the grounds of her pregnancy, which was in the period of sickness and lassitude; she must have been hoping to get through it more easily, in what was usually one of the quieter times of the farm's year. As for her mother's complaint, it seemed to be vindicated when a real calamity occurred, although only part of it was due to the weather. Most of it was caused by the public cattle which had been quartered for the winter on land adjoining the farm.

When Rahiké arrived at the house that day, she found Zoharé the only adult awake. "And as soon as one of the others stirs, I'm off to bed," she said. "Are you here as Young Mistress, or as daughter of the house?"

"As both. If you mean, does Naramethé admit liability, it seems so; though I think it's best if I keep out of it as much as I can. But the Old Mistress seemed to think that at first sight some compensation would be due from public funds. Tell me about it; then I'll go up and have a look."

Zoharé yawned. "We may as well both go; it will keep me awake. The bigger ones are all out of the way now, we'll only have to take Thadek and Rathak. I'll have another look at it; perhaps it will look better than before."

It was a dry morning, with even a hint of sun by the time they reached the western limits of the farm, though small muddy streams were everywhere, delighting Thadek. Surveying the fields, Rahiké could not imagine that her sister found the sight cheering. The boundary wall of the farm had been broken down in a dozen places, banks and ditches between fields had been destroyed, and the fields themselves were a mess of mud and pulpy green, sown indistinguishable from fallow. But the worst damage was to the field before them: it sloped steeply, and the ditch along its top edge, which drained much of the pasture above, had been controlled by a high embankment. No longer: the bank was breached, releasing the water of weeks, and the field glistened with mud. A small flow still trickled from the lowest break in the bank, and found its way down the hillside.

"Well, it is better or worse by daylight?"

"Both. You can see just how bad it is: but at least it's quiet. It was chaos up here in the night. Thick cloud, no moons, rain; black as Nité's arsehole; herdwomen and dogs everywhere, cows bursting out of the dark—and the noise! And I'll tell you, you may think you know a place, but in real darkness you don't. Every trench and stone

turned up before I expected it, or in the wrong place."
Zoharé surveyed the scene again, and groaned. "Of course
by then a lot of them *were* in the wrong place."

"Was this field sown?"

"It was. So was that one with the bush in the middle.
And *that* one was full of winter greens. Some of the cattle
decided to stop running there, and eat. Some others seem
to have broken open a root clamp. But at the time we were
grateful for anything that halted them, whatever they ate:
there were hundreds of them; we feared there wouldn't be
a boundary left standing. And trying, in all the dark and
confusion, to see what needed doing, what could be done.
It was a nightmare."

Rahiké looked across the fields to where, at a little
distance, she could see a cattle compound. "I suppose
that's where they were penned? It looks as if something is
broken there. And that must be the herd, up there?"

"Yes, and I don't know. I didn't care where they took
their precious cattle, so long as it was away, and quickly."

"I wonder what started them off? It must have been
quite a panic."

"No idea. That's the herder's business; and yours, I
suppose."

As they went down they met their mother coming up
with some of the farm women; Rahiké turned back with
them, while Zoharé went on to resign the children to her
great-aunt and take her turn at sleeping. By the time the
Young Mistress reached the house again Mirrik was wan-
dering sleepily about the main room, in a surprisingly
good humor. "I was woken by the *sun*," she said in
disgust. "What an insult; not only sending us foul weather,
but letting it clear as soon as it's done its worst to us."

"Hamathé is appeased by the necessary sacrifice."

"Obviously. Well, what a comfort. Now we can all feel
cheerful about it. Glad to have done our part for the
nation's good."

Rahiké grinned. "Well, I left Mother feeling a bit
better after a promise to get a gang of laborers up to help

with the repairs. And it looks as if the loss on the crops must be made good. It's the embankment that's the worst loss—it may take years for that to be what it was."

"Great-Aunt says her grandmother helped build that as a child; so she was told."

"Who raised the alarm?"

"Sinak; after the dogs, that is. And he spotted first where the trouble was, and was first to identify the noise as cows. *And* he was first dressed and off to rouse the women. This is Sinak's big day; he'll be sure to tell you about it. I won't spoil it for him; you be sure to be around to hear it. What a night, though. You can't imagine the scene up there. I suppose it had its funny side, if it wasn't your farm. Herders cursing cows, farmers, each other— Mother bawling at them to get their beasts out, at the women to plug the bank, at me on no account to lift anything, at Siké not to run the last errand she gave her but another one—me finding corners to puke in—all of us wishing we'd taken the time to put on warmer clothes— dogs chasing cows and children chasing dogs—oh, be glad you were warm in bed."

"I am, I am!"

"At least no one was hurt or drowned; there were so many children come up to join the excitement, I thought in the dark there would be. I'm sure once I saw Zoharé swing two little boys over a wall by their hair; I know I heard them bawling."

"I think two drovers were hurt when the stampede started, but not too badly. One had a dislocated shoulder. I was told she was doing something near the gate; not trying to hold it shut, I hope!"

"Tut, if they will play such rough games—" Mirrik's face grew alert suddenly; she opened the door onto the porch. "Look; here are the twins!"

They were not twins, or even sisters, but cousins born a few weeks apart, raised in the same house, and inseparable from childhood. Mirrik had once had an admiration for them, when she was about thirteen and they

were a few years older; Rahiké, though their age, had
never been one of their circle. She did not dislike them
but she never found them easy company, and even now
followed Mirrik onto the porch with faint reluctance.
There was scarcely a woman in the world who could daunt
Rahiké, but these two could. They were not clever, not
unfriendly, no even especially forceful; just so very different,
so good at what they did, so far from the City.

They had ridden into the space before the porch,
leading another pony, with a pack of dogs behind them
which lay down at a word and rolled their eyes silently at
the farm dogs. Hard brown women, lean rather than slim,
their trousers and smocks made of leather, their hair tied
in plumes from the top of their heads. One had been
talking to Mirrik while she straightened the javelins in her
saddle holster; now she joined her companion, who was
standing with the third pony, and said, "We thought you
would like a look at the cause of your trouble."

They lifted something from the pony and laid it on
the ground; a low reminiscent growl rose from the dogs.
Caught despite herself, Rahiké went nearer. The creature
was a little larger than the largest dog, but much stockier,
blunt faced and velvet pawed; a mountain cat. Its thick
golden pelt, marked with shadows of darker gold, brought
the blaze of summer into the wintry mud of the yard.

"She got into the compound, and made a kill," said
the huntress who had been talking to Mirrik. "No wonder
the cattle panicked."

Mirrik and Rahiké stooped over the animal, the twins
crouched either side of it. The taller of them said, "We
don't know what brought her down so far. She's young and
healthy. She had no excuse, had you, beauty?"

"Well," said the other, "she's paid for her laziness
now."

Rahiké asked, "Aren't they usually like this, then?"

"Not if they come near tame herds; more likely old or
injured—not up to a real hunt. Animals aren't stupid, they
know stealing from women means trouble," She looked at

the Young Mistress with a shyness that was unexpected, ands said, "I always hate killing them then; I'm glad this one was different."

All the while she spoke she was gently stroking the cat's head. Rahiké said, "She is very beautiful."

"Isn't she? You should see the face of a live one—her eyes; how she moves!"

"I'd rather not!"

The other twin laughed. "How'd you like one sitting on your porch? She'd look pretty good, eh?"

Rahiké shuddered. "Her baby sister, maybe!"

The woman stroking the cat said seriously, "You'd need to take a blind kitten, and rear it, and then there's no knowing that it would be tame. The weanlings are as savage as their mothers. But don't ask us how you'd get a kitten. Best stick to dogs. What a lovely pelt; look at it."

I'm looking," said Mirrik. "I wouldn't mind *that* on my porch."

"Hey, hey, we shouldn't have come, Kalliké, such thieves as farmers are! The pelt's ours; go to the lady here for your compensation." She laughed. "Come, let's get her onto the pony again before these two have her skinned and roasted!"

The dead animal must have weighed as much as a calf, thought Rahiké, yet they seemed to have no trouble lifting it onto the packsaddle. Their hands had a hardness unlike that imparted by farm work; the sight of their spears, their bows and quivers, made her uncomfortable. The life of herdswomen must be strange enough, and that of miners; but what could the life of a huntress be? How did a woman come to choose it? How often did these two sleep in a house, bathe in hot water, change their stained leather clothes? And what of the other comforts of those they called "valley women"? What of men? No small part of her unease with them arose from wondering whether they were still virgin. Perhaps they had to be; how could children have a place in their life? Had they no passions, then? No desires? Or how did they spend them?

Mirrik was asking how it happened they were at hand so quickly, and one was saying, "Oh, we were about, we come down for a dish of lentils sometimes," while the other added, "Like the foxes, we come nearer the farms in winter," and they both laughed. Whatever brought them into the valley, Rahiké doubted that it would be bad weather.

She said, "Well, it was lucky for us; and for the herders especially. Mirrik, I must go. It's time to fetch Burdal, and I must report to the Mistress. Tell Mother I'll be back in a day or so, and I'll get some laborers up here tomorrow. As for you, less excitement and more sleep."

"Yes, Madam Rahiké, I'll see to it." The Young Mistress took leave of the huntresses, and glancing back as she left saw them following Mirrik into the house, leaving the little knot of dogs and dozing ponies. They were perfectly normal women, she told herself; not ordinary of course, but only because of their work. Quite well mannered, if not polished, and good-looking in their way: naturally they could not dress like clerks. It was ridiculous to feel parting from them as an escape. But she could never reconcile herself to the wild smell that hung about them, to the sense of space, of silence; of a life that had nothing to do with the domestic world, or with the ordered world of the City.

The weather did not continue kind to the lovers; the frosts returned, the roads hardened, and Rahiké went to Ruthathé. She had never visited it before, and soon wished, despite her welcome, that she had stayed away longer. She returned with a knowledge she found burdensome, and was slow to impart it. Though it concerned Mairilek, and she could not let herself conceal it from him, it was several nights before she found courage to speak of it.

They lay quiet after making love, folded together, her arms about him, his head on her shoulder. There was no sound but the embers falling together on the hearth. Rahiké said suddenly, "They have Lodges of Power in Ruthathé."

She felt his breath deepen, and the sweep of lashes as he opened his eyes, but he did not speak at once. "Do they?". he said at last. "In their Town?"

"No. On their own. West, where the mountains begin." No need to say they seemed to be treated with scant honor. "Perhaps I should not say *Lodges,* I think there is only one." She swallowed; but this was what she had to tell him. "I asked. They take strangers. They would take you."

It was said, and she had only to strive to seem calm. He said nothing for a while, but his fingers pressed harder into her side. She lay staring at the hearth canopy, shaken by her heartbeats. He said, "How far is Ruthathé from here?"

She whispered, "Almost a day's journey. On pony. That is to the City. To the Lodges, I suppose half a day more."

"Three days, then, there and back. Here and back. And that is not walking." He sighed, turning to her and tightening his arms. "It is too far. Anything farther than this is too far."

Rahiké gave a small relieved sob of laughter. Yet what could she have feared? If she found it hard to contemplate such separation, he must find it impossible. At such a moment it seemed easy to be bold; she murmured, "But, Mairilek, perhaps we ought to—I have heard of no other Lodges so close—"

He moved with sudden force, stifling her mouth, pressing the breath out of her with his weight. Halilaki men rarely inflicted their strength on women, even on their lovers, but now his grip was painful, and his kisses hurt. Rahiké gasped with astonishment, and struggled free. Mairilek muttered, "Don't say any more! I don't want to hear. Why do you tell me? Do you want me to go there?"

She gasped again. "Oh, no!" He laughed then, rolling away to lie on his side, and she looked at him indignantly. "What made you so rough?"

"What made you so cruel?"

"I didn't think I was being cruel. I thought—" Then she sighed. "No, I don't want you to go to Ruthathé; or anywhere."

His face half hidden, he grinned at her with one eye and half a mouth. "I didn't think you did."

His confidence in her love often disconcerted her, left her unsure of her reaction to it. Of course he had reason for confidence, but should he be so sure? Did he never feel what she felt too often? Maybe such baseless fears as she suffered were a penalty of that forethought which men escaped. Trust came naturally to them. Now, when her tension had not relaxed, he could widen his muffled grin and add provocatively, "No one ever did."

She buried her fingers in his hair and tightened them, shaking his head not quite roughly. He chuckled. "But I gave the others no choice."

"Tease, tease!" she chided; then, despising herself, asked what she had never yet asked; "Were there many of them?"

She could not keep her voice casual, but he seemed not to notice. "Oh . . . more than there should have been, maybe. No man likes to think that the only women who love him do so for the sake of the child he was. But I got unhappy about it all. There were none for a long while, before you." He moved, and smiled at her in the way that always emptied her of all but joy. "Why: you aren't jealous?"

"Oh, am I not? I'm jealous of every woman who recognizes your name. If ever I hear someone speak kindly of you I can feel my tongue forking."

He stroked her throat. "That is foolish."

"I know. I can't be sensible all the time."

"I will wait to be jealous of the lovers who come after me."

"You will wait a long time, then." She wound a lock of his hair about her wrist, and tugged gently at it. "Tell me, why do I keep hearing how charming you are?"

"You are very unkind tonight. Don't you think I'm charming?"

"Not the way they mean it. Not deliberately charming. Were you?"

She tugged less gently, until he protested and freed himself. "I don't know. Maybe I was; if they mean I wanted to please. I tried hard to be what was wanted, for a while."

"Not with me."

"No. You never made me. And I would not. It mattered that you knew me as I was." He moved back into her arms, saying, "For you not to have loved me would have been bad; but far worse, if I had pretended and you had liked the pretense. If you had loved me for something I was not."

She thought, I am a fool to be jealous. "You thought about it, then?"

"Of course I did. I told you how soon I started loving you. From the evening you offered me the porch, I hoped: but you frightened me. You made me wait so long. I used to dream—no, not dream; I used to plan. All the things I would do to please you, if ever you wanted me, to make you want me again." He chuckled softly. "I don't think I did any of it."

While she had been in Ruthathé, he had finished the work that had been occupying him; a few days later he played it to her. Rahiké called it his river music, for she heard the cold living water run through it all: he demurred a little, but accepted the name after a while, though, he said, that was not how he had been thinking of it. How he had, he did not say. He no longer tried to explain to her what he was doing, or trying to do. She was both sorry and relieved, hoping that it was only that he had decided this was craft-talk and he was doing wrong in trying to share it with a woman. Also she suspected that he found it increasingly hard to put what he knew, what he did, into words. His music was growing difficult even for him. He had to practice long now to execute his ideas, and even longer before he could play his music perfectly. Often it exasperated him that sounds heard in his mind threatened to escape before his hands could capture them. "I forget them before I can play them," he complained, "or I think of more than one, and can't keep hold of them."

"Don't they come back to you?"

"I don't know. Perhaps some. How do you recognize it, if you have forgotten what it was you lost?" She did not say he kept much and lost little; that would be no comfort. "If there were a way to hold it somewhere!" he said. "Like the builders' plans. Or the patterns the weavers draw. I tried drawing patterns once, shaped lines—but when I came back to them, they didn't tell me what I meant when I drew them."

His frustration hurt her. "Who can help you?" she cried. "Who do musicians pray to?"

"Karathek," he said shortly. "Or I do. I am a craftsman, I make for Karathek, I offer him my work."

He sounded out of temper, and she flushed. "I meant, is there a hero? But of course you wouldn't know, I'm sorry."

He smiled apologetically. "There is Ranek the Dancer. I could think of no one more fit. He has a shrine north of the Town, where I go."

"Pray to Ranek, then. Pray to Voiha; I will pray too."

To see him struggling in the net of his ignorance and isolation not only distressed her; it frightened her. It was like the first days again, as if he had only walked a circle. She told herself that she often went through such times herself, when everything seemed tangled and difficult, and that they always passed; but the fear persisted. It was impossible to forget the Lodges of Power in Ruthathé. He never spoke of them, but she was sure they must trouble his sleep as often as hers. Rahiké had not often come to the feet of Voiha; her prayers were offered to Rehera, but now she prayed earnestly, fervently to the Wise Dreamer that a way would be found to help him.

Whether it was Ranek or Karathek or Voiha herself who intervened, he found a way out of one difficulty at least. One evening he came in, very cheerful, and said, "I

have found a way to hold ideas. It is easy. I could have
thought of it long ago if I had kept my temper. Look." He
spread a piece of rough bark-paper before her, and she
stared at the lines marked here and there with crosses and
small upright strokes. "All I have to do is draw a plan of
the strings, and then I can mark which to play and where
to stop them."

"What about the pipe?"

"I can use this too. The only trouble is, it takes a lot
of paper; I have to keep cleaning it. Though I can even
draw it on the ground, if I have to."

She puzzled over it, but not for long. "Well, I can
probably help there; I should be able to get some paper.
But Mairilek, I think I ought not see such things as this. I
think this is for the Lodges, not for me."

Thereafter he often sat bent over scraps of paper,
marking them with charcoal. It seemed a strange way of
making music, and her bewilderment grew again. She had
never liked listening to his explanations, had hated the
useless struggle to understand, but now his silence left her
lonely. At times she felt like one of the legendary women
who had fallen in love with creatures of another element—
river men; or one of Karinané's attendant Immortals,
beings of air and fire. Yet she told herself that all crafts
were mysteries, and that if she saw the process of any of
them and not just the product, she would be baffled.
Mairilek was indeed of another element, another world;
he was a man, a craftsman, a maker, and in that lay all his
strangeness.

Spring came; her courtyard tree, which blossomed
before the leaves grew, covered its dark branches with
pale yellow stars. They opened the porch, and the house
filled with air and light once more. There were days of
festival; the woods clouded green, plants that had seemed
resigned to death tightened their grip on the earth, the
rivers grew loud. Mairilek's river music was put behind

him now. He had begun to make something new, and against his habit he gave this a name: the Spring Song. He had never before announced what an unmade music was to be, and Rahiké took it for another sign of his increased confidence. He trusted himself now to do what he planned. The days grew longer. The birds returned, the vine budded. Young men began to wear flowers in their hair again, and the evenings grew mild enough for them to sometimes sit on the porch.

Mairilek had been born in spring. On an evening not long after his birthday he and Rahiké sat on the porch even after Burdal slept, for the sky was clear and the light lingered. It was growing cool, but after the stuffiness of winter it was not unpleasant to feel the chill, clean air on them. Rahiké said suddenly, "I forgot to ask. How old were you, this birthday?"

He hesitated before he answered; then, "Twenty-four. Do you think I look it? Am I aging?"

He was dressed in summer clothes again, and had made himself a garland of the dark fragrant flowers that were dyeing the stream banks blue. She laughed. But a faint tension rested in his eyes, as if he were waiting; and presently Rahiké repeated, with a changed inflection, "Twenty-four?"

They had drawn the bench near to the porch rail, on which they had been leaning; now Rahiké stood, staring over at the Town. Then she turned to look down at him. "Mairilek," she said, "how long does an apprenticeship last?"

He drew on his pipe before he answered. "It depends how soon your Master thinks you are fit to be a craftsman." He glanced up at her, saw her intense eyes, then looked before him again; and confessed, "At the longest, ten years."

"Ten years! Then—what about you?"

"Oh, I have been the oldest apprentice in the Lodge for years. It's an old joke now; everyone is bored with it. The newest boys call me Uncle, they—"

"Stop it! Be serious! Is this the last year for you, then?"

"Yes."

"Next spring, you won't be an apprentice anymore?"

"No."

She walked about the porch in agitation, while he held his pipe and watched the smoke rise from it. Presently Rahiké came up behind him and put her hands on his shoulders. "Then? Will you be a craftsman?"

He was quiet for a while, then put his pipe aside and laid a hand over one of hers. He said gently, "Rahiké, there is not the smallest chance I would be acceptable. But even if I were—it is not only skill that makes a craftsman."

"What else is there?"

"Well; you know I cannot tell you very much. But there are oaths to be sworn before Karathek; vows I could not make. You know that a craftsman must put his Craft, his Lodge, his Master, above everything. I could not swear that. Not for pottery."

Her hands pressed harder. At last she said, "No. Of course not." He did not move, and she stood still, staring across the valley to the Town. Her voice was empty of expression as she said, "More of my ignorance. Though it concerns the Town, I'm sure I should know, but I do not. I have only heard of Lodge Masters, and Masters, and craftsmen, and apprentices. Nothing else. What do apprentices become, if not craftsmen?"

"Oh, they aren't smothered, or taken out at night and left for the foxes. Nothing like that. No harm comes to them." But she clasped his neck and bent her head beside his, and she cried, "No, *tell* me!" Then he said softly, "Well: there are laborers. They do the rough work."

"What sort of work? Who for?"

"Anything there is. For anyone. Though mostly, they belong to one Lodge more than another. Most Lodges have what they call 'their' men; they—keep an eye on them. I expect I will still work for the Potters' Lodge." He had never before said aloud that he was to be one of them;

he shivered, then turned to Rahiké, putting an arm around her waist and pulling her down to sit on the bench beside him. "Does it matter so much?" he pleaded: "I will still be what I am."

She looked at him distractedly. An apprentice was a son of his Lodge, fed and clothed by his Master, safely housed; but what was a laborer? "But who feeds them? Where do they sleep? How do they live?"

His eyes flinched. He said as if in apology, "They work for hire, so they get their own food. They don't have a proper Lodge, of course, but there is a cabin." He swallowed. "Don't think they are so unhappy. People are kind to them. A lot of them are simple minded." She protested; he said huskily, "Will you make me sleep with the dogs, then? Will it make so much difference to you?"

"To know that you are living like that? In winter, the nights you cannot be here, wondering if you have shelter, if you are warm? Of course it will make a difference! What happens if you are ill, and how can anyone living like that keep well? How will you take care of your hands then? And your music box?"

"I will just have to leave the box here always. I will live. New clothes won't be so easy to come by, of course, and I won't be able to use the Lodge bathhouse. I did warn you I might not always be beautiful. Oh, Rahiké, it won't be so very bad." But she felt his tears, and he muttered, "It will for you, I know. It will be terrible. How they would mock you, if your lover was a laborer. I am sorry. You could not do it."

"Oh, I could!" she said fiercely. "And if I need to, I shall! Let them dare say a word to me!" Yet it was not so simple, and she knew it. A ruler could not be careless of her people's respect. "But Mairilek, this is a long time away. Don't let us weep for it now. It may never happen." She trembled, and cried despairingly, "It shall not happen! There must be some use in being the Young Mistress!"

"Rahiké!" The strength came back into his voice. He looked at her gravely. "Rahiké; my love, my queen; please,

never try to help me so far. This will happen; it must.
Better that than you trying to save me. You could only fail,
you would look a fool. And for me—you could not succeed,
but if you could, I would sooner die, I would die of shame
if you altered what I was in the Town, or if you made the
Town change for me! Do not shame me by trying. Rahiké,
I *beg* you. Whatever I am, it is the Town I have to live
with all my life."

Yet she must think of it. Now she knew the future
that waited for him, her determination to find a way of
helping him grew, though so did her despair of succeeding.
Yet if by some unimaginable persuasion she could bring
the Lodge Masters to listen to her, what would they say?
"You tell us the gift is from Voiha, but the youth is your
lover and he is very fair." Even if they could by anything
less than the intervention of Karathek or a Goddess be
brought to change their ways, what then? If he had a
Lodge, where would his Master be, or his peers? He
would still be alone. And now he had given her another
fear, of what his life might be with all the Town knowing
that the City had intervened for him. They would say it
was his face, not his gift, which saved him. Maybe the
shame really would be intolerable; maybe he would never
forgive her.

At that point she always stopped herself, exasperated.
It was useless to fear the consequences of things that
would never happen, for the Lodge Masters would never
consent. The Laws of Naramethé and of the Town could not
be changed by her, and as they were they would have no
mercy on him. The only hope she could see for him lay in
Ruthathé's Lodges of Power. That thought lay like a stone
under her heart; there must be another way.

The shape of his future cast no shadow into Mairilek's
present. Within a few days of his birthday his heart was as
high as ever; he was not given to looking beyond his task,
and that had become the Spring Song. Day by day it grew,
and added to Rahiké's certainty that he could not go on as
he was, and that if Naramethé made the creator of such a

thing one of the Town's vagrants not only Karathek but all the Goddesses would be offended. It was not the beauty of the music that convinced her, nor the scale, although she became aware that it was more ambitious than anything he had yet attempted; it was watching him as he worked. No other music had enclosed him quite so completely. The Spring Song gripped him, dared him, exalted him. She saw that he knew some greatness to be almost within his grasp. Sometimes when he played a completed passage over she saw his face full of quiet triumph; or as he tested, altered, experimented, she could watch enlightenment dazzle his mind. He began the whole work anew several times, each time with exhilaration; because he had understood more fully what was needed, as the shape of the Immortal emerged from its veils. With this music, when he had not made the sound he wanted, he rarely grew sad or frustrated: he merely turned back, searching for perfection with patient certainty.

The Spring Song he even brought to bed with him. Disturbed from half sleep by the humming of notes in his throat she protested faintly, whereat he woke her completely by scrambling out of bed. She leaned up and saw him crouching over the hearth with one of his pieces of paper, then bending lower to make his marks on the tiles. "Mairilek!"

"Sh!" he said; then, "It will come off. I haven't enough space, and I must not forget this." He picked up both box and pipe before moving back to the bed; she groaned to herself and pulled the quilt about her. He settled himself between her and the wall, his back to the wall, the box on his knees.

"Well, what is this you must not forget, even if it means spoiling the tiles another craftsman made?"

He grinned. "They aren't spoiled. A way to join two things, I hope. Listen."

He played. There were two melodies, one under the other, so it seemed to her. One changed, slanted, tilted down, as the other reached up; they touched as cloud and mountain touch, merged, changed; and the music went on. But it was transformed somehow; it had gained power. Like rivers meeting, she thought; but she would only say, "Like water-pipes?"

"You always compare my music to water. Now it is gutters! All right; I just drew a gutter on your hearth."

She chuckled and linked her hands behind her head. He sat cross-legged, piping; she could feel the weight of the music box against her leg. She remarked, "Apprentice work is a long way behind you now, isn't it?"

"Yes," he said briefly, and played on; then stopped to ask, "Why did you say that?"

"Just, I have been thinking. If you were a craftsman, would the Spring Song be your Master-piece?"

He lowered the pipe and looked thoughtfully at her. "I had not thought of it like that. Maybe it would. Only other Masters could tell me."

"It is special, though?"

"Yes. Even if I fail, if I cannot make it as it should be—it will be a greater thing to have failed at this than anything I have succeeded at. I will have heard it."

"Like a vision," she murmured.

"Except it is in my ears. But I will not fail. I must not. I will bear my child alive." He looked mischievously at her, but she only smiled tenderly. He said with more gravity, "I will make it acceptable to Karathek."

For a moment he was still, withdrawn into another presence; Rahiké's hair prickled. Then he looked down at her and smiled. "What do you mean, '*If* you were a craftsman'? I *am* a craftsman. I am more than that. I have a Power." He began to play again on the pipe, and she closed her eyes. It was part of the Spring Song, but the simplest old lullaby would have sung the heart out of her as surely, if his breath made it live. She reached up and put a hand on his shoulder, saying softly, "Oh, I know. Are you telling me? Do I need to be told what power you have?"

He put the pipe aside and gazed at her, his eyes

glowing in the dim light. She stroked her hand down his arm, and his mouth softened, but it was the music box he reached for, and setting it on his knees he began to play. The box cried sweetly under his hands, and Rahiké felt a piercing sympathy with it. The familiar anguish began. Suddenly as never before the music reached her; its beauty entered her, began to overwhelm her, and her spirit rose up in anger and dread to defend itself. Presently she sat up, her head bowed, not daring to surrender to it. He stopped. Her voice shook: she said, "You wake its soul!"

Maïrilek looked at her questioningly, but his eyes grew startled, meeting the intensity of hers. "You did it to me," she said. "That is what your gift is. You are a waker of souls."

"Rahiké!" he exclaimed, setting the box down. She gripped his arm.

"That box is only wood and wire, the pipe is only a stick with holes in it, but you give them souls, you make them speak. Without you we are all of us dumb."

He put his arms round her, whispering in protest, "Oh, not you, not you!" But she held him away, and insisted, "Yes. I was as dumb as the box once. I mean, inside. Without you my soul does not speak. Naramethé, my work, everything; I did not know how to love them before. You gave them to me."

"That is only because you love me; it is no power I have!"

"But I could not have loved anyone else! Don't you understand?"

He pulled the quilt from between them, covering himself with it as he lay down, and kissed her softly. "Yes, of course I do. Haven't I often said you gave me my music?"

"Perhaps it is the same. I hope so. I don't know." She spoke confusedly. She never found it easy to speak of her feelings, even to him. Words of love came readily to his tongue, but they had to be shaken out of her. He tried now to soothe her, but she drew back, intent on speaking. "Listen. You have been in the Temple of Maha, have you, you have seen the crystals? How they press the light together, and make it brighter, or how they make rainbows? Ordinary daylight; but they don't change it; they don't *make* it so beautiful; they only show it to us. That is what you do. You have shown me. . . . I did not see, I did not hear; I was asleep."

He lay quiet at her side. She leaned against him, and presently grew calmer. Taking his hand and giving a tremulous laugh she said, "I don't tell you often enough that I love you; but when I do I say it loud."

He pushed his fingers up through her hair, but his eyes gazed out beyond her. Soon he said in a low voice, "It makes me afraid. To be so important. I am not strong enough. Only the Gods should be loved so much. Only the Gods are so much to be trusted."

She turned toward him, saying huskily, "You don't feel it, then."

"I do," he said; "That frightens me too."

Some time later he said almost to himself, "But you put Burdal and Naramethé above me." He spoke as if he found reassurance in the thought, but Rahiké did not notice that. "I love them differently," she said. "There is no above and below, no better or worse; only different places."

He sighed. "They are welcome to theirs," he said, "so long as I can have this."

IV

Rahiké had not told anyone of her wish to find a way to save Mairilek from the logic of the law; it was not a matter she wished to discuss, even with Mekiné, who still was unshaken in her belief that Mairilek would be an acceptable potter. Yet the weight became too much to bear alone. There came a day when the Mistress's "A fine morning, successor. How is our lovely boy today?" was not met with the usual light response, but with "Worrying me half to death."

"Ho!" said the Old Mistress, hitching her footstool nearer and eyeing Rahiké with interest. "What is he doing? Giving the eye to one of your sisters? Sulking for presents?"

"No he isn't!" snapped Rahiké. The old woman said soothingly, "I know he isn't, child. I didn't mean it. But what is he doing?"

Rahiké leaned her arms on her table and stared at the marks on the wood. "No, it isn't what he is doing—except that there is this music he is making now—it isn't like the rest; but he isn't doing anything he hasn't always done. It's what he is. What is going to happen to him." She hesitated, but the Mistress said nothing, only watched her. The red bird Rahiké had brought her as a gift from Varaskil clattered the bars of its cage. So she sat back and told it all. When she had done she met the other woman's eyes with a wry smile. There was always a touch of mockery in them, but she saw the sympathy too. "Judgment, Mistress?"

The Mistress stared out into the garden, as she always did when in thought. The red bird swung by his beak, then dropped to the floor of his cage and swore indistinctly. She flicked the bars, saying, "Shut up!" then looked back to Rahiké.

"Well, child, you knew what he was. If you wanted a normal lover, you should not have chosen this one."

Rahiké shrugged and smiled. "I didn't choose to choose him. Anyway, there are better things than normality."

"That's your only answer, successor. What you have doesn't come cheap, and why should it?"

Rahiké leaned over her desk again. "But that is not what worries me. For me, there is no problem. But for him— Has he to spend all his life like this? What will it have done to him by the time he is forty, fifty? You know, Mistress, it is not something I think about often—but there should be people to *listen* to his music. Not only me, but people who would know what it is worth. He says he makes it for Karathek, but I am sure that is not enough. And, next year—they will make him a laborer."

The red bird tutted in disgust, then said in a voice Rahiké knew for her own, "The woman's a fool." She grinned faintly.

The Mistress said, "Perhaps that's the price he has to pay. Maybe he's glad enough to do it; wants to give something for his music?" Rahiké looked at her reproachfully. "Girl, you get angry when anyone calls him a boy, you want him respected as a grown man and a craftsman should be, but yourself, you still want to shelter him from every wind of the world." Rahiké flushed and protested. "All right, not every one, but the cold ones. Rahiké, if he is a man grant him a man's right to make his own choices. Adults accept consequences."

Rahiké muttered, "He can only choose from what is offered. What real choice has he?"

"Ah, well, we all have that problem."

The Young Mistress thought that a woman, especially a self-assured, powerful woman, could have little understanding of his situation. How much did even she understand? What did she really know of his life in the Potters' Lodge?

"Very well; if I accept that, and don't think how wretched it will be, it is going to make his music even harder for him. Even he will think the price too high, if it is that." The Old Mistress pulled a face, but said nothing. Rahiké cried with sudden violence, "Ah, Nité take them all! Damn them, damn the Lodges and their laws! All this fuss about the way to make pots and tables! Why do they have to do it?"

"Steady, successor, steady! Let them live! So maybe we think it is a ridiculous fuss, but it's their world over Nàra. Craftsmanship is their hold on the future, their immortality. Men can't have children, you know; they have to make themselves something else to live for."

"I know; I know. I didn't mean it—don't really mean it. But I get so angry. I feel so trammeled, thwarted—I know: not everything is in our power. Voiha is sleeping."

"Leave the men what the Goddess gave them, Rahiké. She knows, it's little enough."

"Yes, I know." Then she rebelled again, crying, "But they don't even take it all! The men say that only they hear Voiha dreaming—all right, maybe it's true, perhaps that's the reward of a less striving life; isn't that why some women withdraw to Voiha's Precinct? But suppose we believe them, can all the dreams of Voiha be made into chairs and carpets? Yet what Mairilek hears, they will stifle!" Her voice grew fiercer. "If we let that happen—if we let this gift be choked—I think it will be an insult to heaven!"

"Aaaah—now you say it. There is the real worry. I tell you, that disturbs me too, and I don't know what we can do. These gifts are given to the Town. And even you and I can't make Naramethé change so much. Yet here Rehera has sent us something rare; and all we have done with the boy is get hysterical as hens who have hatched a duckling and want to keep it out of the water. As you say, it may be blasphemy. And it is such a waste."

Rahiké burst out, "I hate the music. I hate it. I can't let him know; but I hate the strangeness of it, I hate the way it shuts me out, I hate it for taking so much from him—and oh, I suppose, for what it gives him. But it is a Goddess speaking; I am sure it is a Goddess."

"Then watch your tongue, it is not wise to tell a Goddess of your hatred. Well, then, the matter is in strong hands. Leave it to the Goddess."

"That isn't good enough. What are women for, if the Goddesses have to work with their own hands? They give us a marvel, and we ask for a miracle too?" She drummed her knuckles on the table, then said abruptly, "They have Lodges of Power in Ruthathé. He could go there. I told him about them. But he won't listen." A small smile curved her face. "He never talks about them. He got quite angry when I brought the subject up."

The Old Mistress gave one of her unnerving cackles. "Oh, then, he's lost! Whenever a man of mine started swearing he could never think of leaving me I knew it was time to get a new smock and go courting again!" She glanced at her successor and relented. "No, but your boy isn't like that. Town and City know, he thinks Maha only made the world for you to live in it. All the same, Rahiké. Ruthathé. It's worth thinking about."

"I know it is," she said gloomily.

The Mistress laughed again. "We would have to teach him to ride—that will shock Nehsa!—and give him a good pony; that is all, girl. Fire of Maha, enough, though!"

"He won't hear of it." But she sighed. "Not now. But maybe when his apprenticeship has to end—anything is better than sleeping under porches, or whatever they do."

"He wouldn't need to stay in Ruthathé for ever," said the Old Mistress. "Who knows? A few years, when he is a Master—and I suppose there is no doubt of that—and if there *is* a Goddess with him; maybe if he brought his

Power back to Naramethé then, the Town would not refuse him." She spoke with energy, but their eyes met ruefully; they both knew that he could be a Master in Ruthathé, even in Halkal-Mari, and Naramethé would keep to its old opinion of him. Rahiké sat up and lifted a box of papers onto her table.

"Well, it won't be until next spring. It gives me time to get hardened to the idea. Maybe get braver. And anything may happen in that time. Voiha may wake before next spring."

Burdal turned five. She was growing independent; she needed no escort now to her grandmother's farm, nor to the Children's Court, but made such journeys with only Heffa at her side. Her adoration of Mairilek had grown quieter, though not less; he was woven into the fabric of her life. She demanded that he make a music to mark her birthday. Rahiké scolded her, saying that he was busy with his Spring Song, but he was amused: "Do you think I can only do one thing at a time, then?" He made Burdal her music; it was a return to the days when he had played only tunes, a bright dancing melody, simpler than anything he had made for months. He even taught Burdal to play it for herself on the strings, although it was richer when he played it. Rahiké loved it: he thought she did so because it was for the child, and she did not tell him that she was delighted by its merry simplicity.

Early in summer he came one evening dressed in his best, wearing his favorite jewelry and with white flowers in his hair. There were even traces of paint about his eyes. Rahiké exclaimed to see him so fine, "Where is the festival?"

"Here," he replied, and laughed at her puzzled look. "I thought you would not remember. It's a year ago tonight that you stopped sending me back to the Lodge."

"Oh, Mairilek!" She was touched; he said, "One year behind us, and forty before!" The Halilaki, an optimistic race, had no sense of a malign fate that waited to punish such speeches. "Unless you mean to turn me away when my hair is gray?"

She smiled at the thought of him with gray hair, then found the picture, after all, very pleasing. His face would be thinner, maybe, finer; or would it strengthen with age, grow majestic? "I am likely to go gray before you."

"You aren't so much older."

"No; but so much more careworn."

It was high summer before the Spring Song was finished. He played it to her one evening, and she sat on the stairs gazing across the valley at the group of trees and rocks that all her life would bring such moments back to her, gripped by the familiar pain. Now she heard it complete, even she could hear how remarkable it was. There was a hardness to it, a fine balance, a sheen.

It was never she who broke the silence after he played; but when he spoke this time he only said, "My arms ache." Then he put his instrument down on the bench, sighing, and came to sit on the steps behind her. Usually he invited her judgment in some way, but that night he only stared silently before him. At last she glanced up at him.

"It is good, isn't it?"

He nodded slightly. "I think so. Anyway it is as good as I can make it."

"I hope it pleases Karathek."

"So do I."

"And you?"

He sighed again. "I don't know. It doesn't seem to matter. I've cared so much about it for so long, yet now I can't care at all. It has left me. I don't feel anything. Only tired."

Rahiké looked at him, and for the first time could see how he might look when his youth was gone. He leaned against the rail, his eyes closed, his hands slack between his knees. He looked spent. This music had taken life from him.

She burned with resentment and grief. "It costs you so much!" she said. "What is it for?"

He opened his eyes and smiled. "What, the music?"

She nodded. "What is it worth, that it should take all it does from you? I know it is beautiful, but is that enough?"

"It is for me." He yawned. "That is a question for a Master. What is the purpose of music? I don't know. I am only a craftsman, content to make." In a while he said more seriously, "I have told you, I make for Karathek—for my work to be acceptable to him. Must everything have a use? Is beauty not enough on its own? Do you think I have added nothing to the world?" He hesitated. "What is it for? I have wondered too. You said to me once, 'This is part of Voiha's dreaming.' I pray that it is, for if it is anything less than that it is nothing. But, there is one thing I have thought. . . . Craftsmen, and women, they are the makers and the rulers; they touch the world and they change it. But could there not be something else? To—praise it? Though that is not the word. As we acclaim the Gods. We do not change them by that; it *does* nothing, but it is our duty all the same." He moved his feet thoughtfully. "Sometimes a craftsman's work has made me see things I had not seen; the shape of a tree, the way a dog crouches—I should like to do that. It seems to me a bigger thing than making a thing for use only. I would like to make people hear; or make them listen, at least. All the earth makes music, and who hears it?" He looked earnestly at her. "Is that sensible?"

"To reveal the world. To celebrate it." It was a new notion of a craftsman's duty. He nodded.

"But Rahiké, I don't do what I do because I think that. I would do it anyway. The reasons are for Karathek. I only do what he has made me to do." After a pause he added softly, "It must cost me something, or it cannot be a worthy offering. And the more it costs, the more worthy it will be. If I make well enough for my work to be acceptable to him, then he will accept me as his craftsman."

Rahiké sat still, understanding his hope at last. While she schemed, he worked on, in the quiet humble trust of the Town; and beside that all her plans looked foolish. She thought, Have I been trying to interfere, have I been too busy? Karathek is the God, after all; one of the Children of Maha. And I, have I been trying to come between him and his craftsman? Shame crept over her. It had taken her too long to learn respect for men, but she learned it at last.

She said humbly, "You have more faith, in the Town, than we have. I always want to give the Goddesses a nudge. If I had been there when Maha made the world, I would have been saying, 'You've missed a bit over there.'" He laughed, sitting up straighter. She touched his foot lightly. "Karathek must surely accept such worship."

She went to fetch some wine and their pipes. The dusk grew deep and clear, like a blue jewel, and Maha lit the small fires of the night. Mairilek said after a silence, "You do think it is good?"

She replied quietly, "Surely you know by now, my opinion is not worth having. If you make it, it seems marvelous to me; but you need another Master to give you his judgment. To me, yes, it seems remarkable. More people ought to hear it." Suddenly she spoke with more energy. "Well, and why shouldn't they? If I gathered some of them here, the Mistress, other people, would you play to them? It's time more people learned what you are doing."

He nodded, but yawned again. "Of course I would, if you wished it. Only not yet. I don't feel I want to make any music for a while. Especially not that."

Rahiké had rarely been within the precinct of the Temple of Wise Voiha. She had only been to worship in the quiet empty Temple itself, and that not often; although she gave the Dreamer proper reverence, she was Rehera's servant.

The grounds of the Temple were large and peaceful, and very lovely, though unkempt. There everything was left to grow in its own way, a strange sight in Halilak where even the woods were tended. Now, late in summer, even the most well-used paths were all but drowned in grass and flowers. As she drew nearer to the Temple and the Priestesses' quarters, she passed some of the huts of the anchorites who spent all their lives here. They were of both sexes, women and gentle, bearded men, the only unshaven men she had ever seen.

The Old Mistress had asked her to take a messsage to the High Priestess, but Rahiké was not able to see her and had to leave a letter with her servant. She went back through the grounds again, but by a different path. "If you go past Vanek's Garden you may see her there," the Mistress had said; and out of habit Rahiké had replied, "Oh, you mean the Dreamer's House?," although she knew quite well what the Mistress meant. The lunatic who had lived among such strange visions that the Mantle of Voiha had been put out to shelter her had been dead for some years, but Rahiké and all her generation still called the house by her name, as the women of the Mistress's age still spoke of the inhabitant their youth had known. Rahiké looked there for the Priestess, but the house and garden were empty.

The Young Mistress was halfway back to the City when she stopped in the road and gasped aloud. The Mantle of Voiha. How had she, in all her hopeless scheming, never remembered this? She had talked of the Wise Dreamer, had declared that Mairilek's music was part of Voiha's dreaming; she believed it; yet she had never thought of looking for help to the Wise Goddess or those who served her. No law of City or Town could touch those whom her Temple chose to shelter. Why had she not remembered?

She laughed aloud, dazzled with hope. The first two people she remembered as having come under the Mantle were not encouraging examples, true, for the Dreamer had been mad in the world's eyes at least, and the other had been a woman condemned for blasphemy; but she was sure there had been others, neither lunatics nor criminals. The Vanek of the Mistress's day, surely, had been a craftsman rejected by his Lodge; a sculptor, if the strange carvings around the garden were his work. Might not the High Priestess be willing to stretch the Mantle of Voiha over Mairilek? If she did, neither the women nor the craftsmen could do other than respect it. This was a way that he himself might be willing, even glad, to take. In the Temple he could not have the companions that a Lodge could give him, but he would not be secluded; he could have friends, he could be her lover still without scandal— without too much scandal: and all his life he would have liberty to work, with safe and honorable provision. He could even visit the musicians in Ruthathé if he wished, going and returning as he pleased; he would be free of all demands and restraints.

Rahiké's violent excitement felt like panic. Wait, wait, she thought; am I being too busy again? Will he want to trust to Karathek alone? But who could divide Karathek from Voiha? And if she were overreaching, the old Priestess would tell her so. She could only bring his name, his situation, to her notice. Anything else would not be her doing. The Mantle was not put out at any bidding save that of the Goddess. It was rarely put out at all. It was not certain that Mairilek could live within it; but there was hope, a better hope than any she had ever thought to see.

She sat by the road and wept, careless of who saw her, though it was years since she had wept openly; and when her tears were spent she almost turned back to the Temple to seek the High Priestess at once. Then she checked herself; had she not just found that the Priestess could not be seen? Besides, her day's work was not finished, and the Mistress expected her back. She went on her way to the City, and as she walked she decided that it was better in all ways not to be precipitate. She would wait, and let the idea settle in her mind. There might be reasons against it she had not seen. She would not talk of it at all, least of all to Mairilek; she would wait. It was proverbial that the Dreamer's votaries must learn patience before all else. There was time yet, the rest of summer, all autumn, all winter. Though she would not wait so long as that. She had a journey to make soon, to Sikas. When she returned, then she would seek out the High Priestess of ·Voiha.

Mairilek grumbled when he heard she was going away again, but it was habit, without particular force. He knew that as the Young Mistress's lover he had to accept that her duties would often, and increasingly, come between them; and their past and future now seemed long enough to him for them to spare a few days to the rest of the world. "Will you ride there?"

"Yes. Sikas is a little too far to walk. I will take my little brown pony again. At least, I hope Nehsa will give me that one; we get along together."

"You must be quite a good rider, now."

"I wouldn't say good, and I don't think Nehsa would. Competent, with all the practice I have got this last year or so."

"Do you think if you go to Halkal-Mari again you will ride there?"

"There would be no point; the caravans go at walking pace. Besides, I'd have baggage; I'd be better with the donkey cart. The pony is for when there's not much to carry but me."

He stretched his arms along the window frame and sighed, leaning back, stretching out his legs. Even in the shade of the porch, it was gaspingly hot. Rahiké looked at him, amused by his languor. The music box lay neglected at his side; the heat had even sapped his inclination for music. Indeed, he had not really recovered from the weariness the Spring Song had left in him. He played and he practiced, but he had not yet begun any new music.

He had tanned to the light, clear brown that became him best, and the heat laid a faint damp sheen on his skin. He had cut his hair, despite her protests, but she admitted now it became him best only reaching his shoulderblades. His face was tranquil, but not relaxed out of any expression; his eyes brooded on the shimmering valley. It was rarely now that his beauty became so vivid to her, and a delight when it did. She rocked her chair back, then reached out a foot and prodded his leg. "How dare you say 'if' I go to Halkal-Mari again! Don't you know I was born to be the confidante of Queens?"

He turned to smile at her, saying, "I know you were," with such serious fervor that she colored a little. He asked, "How long will you be away in Sikas?"

"Five or six days at the most."

"And when are you going?"

"In eleven days."

"Eleven days?" He grew more alert. "Oh, that's not so bad. I could not have seen you then even if you were here." She regarded him indignantly, and he looked amused. "Do you think we are fools? We can count, if we can't read. I know what phase of the moon to watch for nearly as well as you do."

Rahiké had not remembered until he pointed it out that her time of bleeding would come during her absence, and not until she was on the road did she realize that there might be some inconvenience in paying tribute at such a time. Sikas was ruled by a Queen, and if report were true this lady was always attended by a group of youths chosen for their beauty. The Young Mistress could hardly ask her to dismiss her train before she came into her presence. She scowled a little. Maybe they were young boys, not of apprentice age; but she did not think so. They would be men in law, and she must avoid them. That would delay her business and lengthen her absence.

Queens by descent were not common in Halilak. In most lands authority was something to be bestowed on a woman, not a possession she was born to inherit. The people of such places, like Rahiké, thought it odd and foolish that a woman should rule not because of what she was but who. Halkal-Mari's glory was perhaps most fitly

embodied in a Queen, who was in any case served by
many advisors; the Priestess-Queens derived their authority
justly from their dedication to the Great Goddess; and in
some places they called their elected rulers Queens; but
there were women who thought all these impious. Rehera
was Queen of Earth, for she had come out of the belly of
Maha; but no mortal woman had the right to such a title.

Sikas was no larger than Naramethé, but its ruler
kept good state in her little court. Rahiké was received as
befitted a royal guest, heir to a sister ruler; waited on in
her luxurious little guest-house, even in her bath, which
was a new experience for her, and then conducted to the
feast made in her honor with a degree of ceremony that
would have disconcerted many women not accustomed to
such usage. Rahiké rather enjoyed the novelty. She did
not covet a dignity that could never be put aside, and the
Queen did not seem to be a woman of such ability as to
lessen her doubts about inherited power; but she was a
courteous hostess, the royal children made a pretty row,
and the young attendants had been well enough chosen for
even Mairilek's lover to enjoy looking at them. She felt
her visit had begun well.

The bleeding did not come next morning when she
looked for it; she put it down to the heat and the ride, and
thanked Veraha for a day's grace, then for two. It was not
until the third day it occurred to her that maybe she
should be thanking her for something else.

She was working alone in the sitting-room of the
guest-house when the thought came to her, and she sat up
abruptly, swinging her legs off the couch, scattering papers
from her lap. "Oh, Great Rehera!" she said aloud, then
flinched guiltily when she heard the reproach in her voice.
She pressed her hands against her belly, as if she expected
to feel some change. Could I be pregnant? she asked
herself; and answered impatiently, Of course I could! I
have had a lover for five seasons. Women who spend all
their time among the beehives tend to get stung sooner or
later.

Then she was sorry again to be thinking in such a way, so ungracious, so ungrateful. She should be full of hope and delight, and all she could feel was dismay. She raised her hands in submission, saying, "Forgive me, Veraha!"; though it was apology, not penitence. But a moment later she was moved with compassion; setting her hands over her womb she said with real compunction, "Forgive me, child, if you are there."

That thought changed her mood. For a long time now she had thought of pregnancy only as an affliction that would banish Mairilek from her arms, and the end to be longed for as his return rather than the birth of a child. She had thought of the possible baby with resentment, as an intruder in her body; but now when she spoke to it, it was not the same. She felt no sudden welling of love, but she did feel pity, and kindliness. "I did not love Burdal before she was born, you know," she explained. "I was pleased and excited, but I did not love her until I knew her. You will be as dear to me in time as your sister."

Your sister. This involved other people beside herself. It was not something a year would end. Her life was altered forever, and so was Burdal's, and Mairilek's. For a moment the sense of panic returned, and the grief. Tears filled her eyes. "O, Mairilek, it will never be the same again!" she cried. Then she swallowed, and took command to herself. She picked up the scattered papers and began to sort them, thinking, I am reacting too soon, far too soon. It might not be so; this is early to be sure. But in her heart she had no doubts.

By the time evening had come she had made herself once more only the Young Mistress of Naramethé, and all her possible pregnancy meant was that there need be no disturbance or delay in her work; she need not avoid the presence of men. At the Queen's table that night she learned another reason to be glad of that. The Queen said to her, "We will have a pleasure tomorrow that comes only rarely, Madam Rahiké, and it is fortunate indeed that it happens while you are our guest. I am told that the musicians who pass this way sometimes have come today."

The Queen had hoped to please her guest by the news, but Rahiké's delight and interest were greater than she had expected, and more gratifying. "They are fine musicians," the Queen said. "I believe that their home is in Halkal-Mari, or that they pass their winters there. But in summer they travel around. They come this way most years; have they never visited Naramethé?"

"Even if they are the ones that I remember, they have not done so for many years. They might well feel they would not be welcomed. Musicians are not honored in my land. We have no Lodges of Power."

The Queen raised her brows and laughed. "Oh, nor have we!" she said. "The musicians are skillful men, no doubt, and it is a pleasure to hear them sometimes; but who would wish to see her son such a man?"

"A vagabond; a vagrant," agreed the woman on Rahiké's other side. "They belong nowhere, they live under no laws. You will see, Madam Rahiké." She shook her head, and uttered the darkest denunciation Halilak knew. "They are homeless men."

All the women to whom Rahiké spoke of the musicians next day talked of them in the same way, looking forward to the entertainment but disparaging the men. She felt sad and indignant. They are no better than us, she thought. One would think these men were performing dogs. Is there no one else like me, who hates music but respects musicians?

That day in the shrine of Rehera she added another to her prayers: the child she had perhaps conceived. She had grown gentler toward it, and if she felt no tenderness she felt responsibility. It had a right to her prayers. And as she prayed, she remembered Mairilek saying, "Would a son of yours be only another child to me?" She had not thought until then that he might come to love the baby, as Tirek loved Mekiné's children. For the first time she felt some pleasure in the idea of her pregnancy. She might have a son; the notion of a little boy was appealing, and made this child seem less of a rival to Burdal. Every girl should have a little brother.

It was rare for women in Naramethé to gather together for meals, and to sit down every evening with so many others was a curious experience for Rahiké. The youths attending the Queen did not eat, yet their mere presence seemed slightly improper. Rahiké wondered if they belonged to Lodges, or if their apprenticeships could not begin until the flower of their beauty had begun to fade; and she determined to ask at another time. That evening all her attention was on the musicians.

They did not come in until the feast was over. The tables were removed, more benches were placed, and women who had not been at the meal crowded into the room. Then the musicians entered. Their appearance startled Rahiké, and the woman who had called them vagabonds gave her a knowing smile. The men of Halilak were indoor creatures, careful of their looks and conscious of their charm, even late in life fastidious in their grooming. Women rarely saw them at work, and Rahiké was accustomed to men, especially young men, looking always smooth, trimmed, polished. These men were weather-beaten, roughened; clean enough, though not with the freshness of those who bathed daily, but brown as farmhands. Their clothes were good, if not fine, and one or two wore jewelry; but not one of them, though most were young and some were almost boys, had dressed his hair, painted his eyes, or made himself a garland. They reminded Rahiké of the Twins, except that their appearance suggested not hardiness but neglect; they had the dingy toughness of stray dogs. Most shocking of all, they were bearded. In Halilak men shaved right to their hairline, partly to keep the appearance of boys as long as possible but chiefly because of the belief that a beard sapped a man's virility. Some criminals were compelled to go unshaven, and the men in Voiha's precinct chose to do so; Rahiké had seen no other bearded men, and the sight of these repelled her.

At first, their music was disappointing. It was not that she did not enjoy it; indeed, she enjoyed it more than much that Mairilek played. The variety of instruments and sounds was interesting, and she was pleased to find that several musicians sang and one was a singer only; yet most of the time she listened, thinking, Is this all? Their music grew less simple as the evening passed, but none of it awed her as her lover's did, and not all the players had his skill. Then their leader, who had been standing near the back of the room, came through his companions to stand before the throne.

He was a burly man, and the outdoor hardness was most marked in him. His kilt and waistcoat were of leather, and while most of the young men had trimmed their beards close to their jaws, his grew thick, hiding his neck. He saluted first the Queen, and then Rahiké; something about the Young Mistress caught his attention, and he looked at her again. Rahiké found his glance startling, without knowing why; it was not only his ugliness. The young musicians placed a stool for him; then, they seated themselves in an arc on the floor. Three instruments stood waiting. The musician picked up one of them, and began to play.

This time Rahiké knew she was listening to a Master. The skill in his hands was wonderful, and the music he played was like that her lover made, music which made her bend her head and long to shut her ears against it. He played on the frame of strings, on a big-bellied instrument with a bent neck that rested over his shoulder, and on a coiled tube of metal. The broken-necked instrument made a deeper, softer sound than the frame, and the voice of the tube was so mild and sweet that she lifted her head to hear it. This was a great craftsman. Yet it seemed to Rahiké, listening to him, that any distance between him and Mairilek was much less than the distance that separated them both from the other players. He was an eagle among falcons; yet hearing him Rahiké grew more than ever sure that Mairilek too was an eagle. Long before he finished playing her mind was filled with only one thought, which governed her through the rest of the performance and the courtesies that ended the evening, which stayed with her until she slept and waited for her when she woke. Mairilek must meet that man, she vowed: Mairilek must hear him.

She sent a message to him next morning, for that was to be her last full day in Sikas; and in the afternoon, when she and her hostesses had parted to rest through the hours of greatest heat, he came seeking her. She went onto the porch to greet him, and he stood before it, a stocky figure, still wearing his leather clothes despite the heat. He met her eyes direct and unabashed, without the deference she expected from men, so that she was surprised and almost offended, but his bearing was not insolent. "Madam Rahiké?" he said, and bowed when she acknowledged it. "I am told you want to speak to me."

His voice was unusual, not so much deep as strong and resounding; there was a ring to it she had never heard before. She studied him a moment. His face was less ill-favored than she had supposed, despite the disfiguring beard, and he was not quite so old as she had first thought, although his hair was graying. His hands caught her attention, not for any beauty they had, rather because they were the only thing about him which seemed well cared for.

"I did, Master Musician. I am the Young Mistress of Naramethé, which lies south and west of here. Tell me, is your journey planned? Does it take you north or south?"

He looked keenly at her when she called him Master. The fearlessness of his stare startled her again. He said, "In spring we go north, in autumn south. We walk the roads now toward Halkal-Mari, but we are at liberty and go where we please."

That was the quality that disturbed her in his manner:

independence. "We have never seen you in Naramethé," she said.

He answered, "When we leave Sikas, our habit is to take the road that passes through Karserik."

"Then you have passed east of us in other years. If your journey took you to Naramethé, you would be welcome."

He inclined his head politely. "That is good to know." Suddenly she laughed.

"That is not what I meant to say. Master, I sent for you to ask you: Will you come to Naramethé? It is very long since musicians came to us, and I think such musicians as you are not often heard anywhere, save perhaps in Halkal-Mari."

He smiled. "Madam, there is nothing so sweet to a craftsman as praise, nor so likely to draw us where more is to be had. Unless my companions refuse, we will come to Naramethé."

"But it is the praise of their peers, I believe, that craftsmen find sweetest? And I fear my country is not a place where you would expect to find your equals. Yet though there is no Musician's Lodge in our Town, some of our people would be glad to—know more—of you."

She had meant to say "of your mystery," but her courage had failed her. Still, her voice had slowed on her last words, and she thought from his look that he guessed there was some unspoken meaning. It was better so. She did not wish to go nearer to Mairilek. He would not want her to lead him by the hand to this man.

When Rahiké told the Mistress of the invitation she had given, she was disconcerted by the incredulous stare she received. "Asked a troop of musicians to come here? Have you run mad, successor?"

"Holy Fire, have I done wrong? I didn't think you would object."

"Object? I don't object. Visitors are always interesting,

well worth anything they cost. Anyway, if I give you authority I expect you to use it. But you have gone mad, all the same. What made you ask them?"

The Young Mistress wished she had left telling of it until morning. She was dusty and stiff from her ride, longing for a bath and Burdal. "Oh—we haven't heard musicians here for ten years at least. And I happened to hear these, and they are very good, especially their leader. You know I am interested, Mistress."

"You? You hate music, you told me so. You did it for that boy of yours, I know." Rahiké laughed, and the old woman snorted. "A good thing there are others who will enjoy listening, or I might object to buying him presents out of public money." But there was no sting in her words. Rahiké said, "Wait till you hear them. And think of the news they will bring, from all over Halilak. Besides, they go to Sikas and Karserik; why should Naramethé be ignored?" She gathered up her belongings to go. The Mistress eyed her with gloomy perplexity.

"Perhaps you need a new sunhat."

"What do you mean?"

"It's making a journey in this heat. You've been in the sun too long. It's turned your wits. Bringing musicians here!"

Rahiké only laughed, thinking it no more than mock grumbling, and took her leave. The Old Mistress watched her go and muttered, "Mad, mad." Her red bird whistled and she turned to him, reaching for his dish of nuts. "You're a lovely thing," she told him, "and if you want nuts you can have them; but your cage stays shut, do you hear? You aren't getting the wind under *your* wings."

Rahiké did not tell Mairilek of the invitation to the musicians, fearing to raise his hopes. It was quite likely that they would decide not to change their plans that year, but to come to Naramethé in the next. Nor did she tell him of her suspicion that she had conceived. There was no need for him to know before he must, before she was certain.

An opportunity to visit the High Priestess of Voiha did not come immediately, but she was not anxious to create one. If she went to the Temple with no known cause, all Naramethé would be speculating on her reason; she did not want that, nor questions from Mairilek. After all, there was no hurry. Harvest would soon be beginning. That always provided reasons for visiting everyone. She would go during Harvest, and after it she would bring together some people to hear him play, as she had suggested to him. Her birthday would offer a good pretext; after all, she would be thirty, she would make an occasion of it. In that way the High Priestess could hear him without it seeming conspicuous. It was good, too, that if the musicians did visit, they would have something with which to compare his playing. She congratulated herself on the way events were shaping, and walked with a higher step. She could almost see the Goddess's Mantle opening for him.

The musicians did come. They arrived only six days after her own return from Sikas, going first to the Town to ask hospitality of the craftsmen. Then, while the younger men settled into the Guest Lodge, one of the Lodge Masters brought their leader to the Mistress. Rahiké was not in the Mistress's House when he came. She returned to it just as the two men were leaving, and seeing the unmistakable figure of the Master Musician she hurried toward them with an exclamation of pleasure. The Lodge Master insisted on presenting the visitor to her with proper ceremony; it amused Rahiké a little to see him showing all the respect due to a fellow Master. She thanked Master Harinel for his introduction, and said, "I am fortunate in having already heard Master Sarak play. I am glad, Master, that your journey lay this way."

"I also, Madam Rahiké: and I regret we cannot stay longer. We can spend only two nights here." Rahiké exclaimed in dismay, and he spread his hands sorrowfully. "I wish it were not so, Madam, but my companions reminded me of what I had forgotten: that we had given our word to be in Karserik before Harvest. Tonight we must rest, tomorrow night we shall play for you, and the next day we must go."

She said, "Then we must hope to welcome you for longer in another year, and be glad you could come at all."

He smiled. "Oh, we wished to come. Also," he said, and he gave her his strange, keen look, "if my companions had not wished it I would have persuaded them. It is worth some trouble to play again before you, Madam Rahiké. I have a great curiosity to know why a lady who I could see took little pleasure in our music was so eager for us to visit her country."

Rahiké did not blush, but she looked conscious. "You are mistaken, Master Sarak. I listened with great enjoyment, and I wished Naramethé to share my pleasure." He smiled skeptically, and bowed as she took her leave. The Lodge Master led him away. She watched them go, thinking that before he reached the Town his great curiosity would be satisfied.

It was a considerable disappointment that they would only stay so short a time. She had hoped they would be in the Town for days, that Mairilek would have many opportunities to talk to them. Now, there would scarcely be time for him to meet the Master; unless he did so that same evening.

He did not. He came to her. She had looked for excitement, but he seemed only shocked. She had pictured him springing up the stairs, imagined the eager ring in his voice; but he came slowly and spoke hoarsely. There was no smile about his mouth or eyes, and his pallor yellowed his tan.

"Rahiké," he said as he came into the house. "Rahiké: there are musicians in the Town."

"I know; I have seen their Master." She looked at him, concerned, suddenly unsure how he would take her next words. "I asked them to come here, Mairilek. I heard them in Sikas; and I invited them here." He stared at her, and sat down on the window seat. She looked at him in perplexity. "Mairilek, what is it? I hoped you would be pleased." Her voice dropped. "Are you angry that I interfered?"

"No, no." He shook his head. "Only I can't believe it. I had been at the clay pits all day, and—I came back and they told me, the Guest Lodge was full of musicians." He moved his hands across his face, then looked up at her. "*You* asked them to come here? Why?"

"So that you could meet them, of course!" she cried. "The Master, their Master; I want you to hear him play. I want him to hear you. I want you to talk to him! Don't you *want* to meet them?"

"Yes: I do. I do," he muttered. He gazed at her again. "And *you* brought them. You give me everything."

"Mairilek, stop this! What is the matter with you? Do you want some wine?"

He laughed faintly. "I think I need some." She rose to fetch it. He rubbed his face again, and dragged his fingers through his hair. "Rahiké, I never had such a shock. It is half my lifetime since I heard a musician. I never thought to hear one again." His color was returning. "And now, eight of them!"

"You never heard a musician like this one before," she asserted, handing him a cup. "Well, and when you heard, what did you do?"

"I went to the bath house." He looked defensive. "I told you, I had been at the pits; I was filthy." He drank, and shook his head. "Then I went down to the Guest Lodge. I thought, I will greet them anyway. They were all on the porch. I *meant* to speak to them—to the young men at least—and then I saw them. I, I felt sick. I couldn't go near them."

"But you must!"

"I know I must! I will! But—they were talking together; carrying instruments; I couldn't go near them, couldn't talk to them. I came here." He drank again, and managed to smile. "Maybe it was the beards."

"Of course it was not." She had not foreseen this; she considered, pouring herself some wine. "Mairilek, the young ones do not matter. You are better than them anyway. It is the Master you must see. And soon; they cannot stay long, only two nights. See him tonight. Mairilek, go back now and look for the Master. He may have heard of you by now; he may be expecting you!" But he shuddered, and said, "No, not tonight. They will be resting tonight."

"Tomorrow, then, in the day."

"They will be practicing then!"

She knelt before him and shook him. "Mairilek, they have come here, out of their way, because I asked; and it was only so you could meet the Master. You must, you must go to him. What is the matter?"

He set down the winecup and hid his head between his hands. "I am terrified!" he cried.

She sat back on her heels and stared at him. The warmth was coming back to his face, but there were tears in his eyes. "I am terrified. Oh, I thought if ever a musician came near me I would romp up to him—you thought so too; but it is not like that! There they are—they are companions, a craft brotherhood. How do I speak to them, what do I say? And this man, their Master. You tell me he is a great musician; and I am to force myself on him, tell him I am a musician too, make him listen to me? Rahiké, for the first time in my life I feel like a potter!"

He swallowed, drawing his hands down his cheeks, and shook himself. "It's more than that, too. Shame; if I could not bear a little shame for my work, Karathek would never own me. But, the worse thing: these men are musicians. They *know*. Suppose I play to them, and— Oh, Rahiké! If what I have done—if they tell me I am not a musician!"

He grasped her shoulders. She covered his hands and watched him while he calmed himself. "And yet: musicians in the Town!" he said. "How I have prayed for it. This is like Voiha waking. We say we hope for it: but if it were to happen!"

"Mairilek, you must see the Master," she said steadily. "I understand why you are afraid. But believe me, you are

as good as—better than—any of those young men. You *are*
a musician. You know you are. You do; you will believe it
again soon. This is only shock. But, whether you feel sure
of yourself or not, you *must* go to the Master. You must
play to him!" She imagined how poor a thing even the
Spring Song must seem to him now—all his festival clothes
turned to tatters. "If for no other reason, then go because
I ask it. You will go?"

After a moment he nodded, and tried to smile. She
stroked his hair.

"Why not go tonight?"

But he said again, "No, they will be resting tonight.
No." He stretched his arms to her. "I am not brave enough
yet. Give me some courage, Rahiké; you have given me
everything else."

She gathered him close, thinking to offer comfort; but
that was not what he wanted, not what his caresses asked.
The flames lit in her blood, and her embrace changed. He
muttered, "I can't go tonight. I need to be with you
tonight."

Rahiké was bewildered by the desperation of his
passion. "I want you with me, you know I do," she
whispered. "Not tonight, then. This is early for bed.
Come to bed." As they stood his embrace did not loosen,
nor his kisses stop. She heard his whispering, and felt his
tears; she sobbed faintly and tried to move, saying, "Yes,
yes; come and lie down." It was what she thought he said:
but the muffled words had been, Oh, what have you done?

Not all those who came to listen to the musicians
were moved by a desire for music; most were gathered by
curiosity or the love of an occasion, while some came
only to assert their right to a place at any assembly. The
Assembly House in the Market, though large, was not
large enough to hold them all, but Rahiké had made sure
of a private place for Mairilek in the recorder's booth over
the door. She looked up to it when she took her place, and

saw him there, leaning back in the shadow. She smiled, but his eyes were downcast and he did not see.

The benches were almost entirely filled with women. Few men could find places, though room was made for the Masters, and some of the more distinguished craftsmen sat along the narrow gallery. The porches were crowded with those who could not get inside. The Young Mistress thought that while they might not hear so well they had the greater comfort, for though all the doors stood open and the shutters were raised, even the traps in the roof, the great room was uncomfortably warm. It made Rahiké drowsy. She had been heavy-headed all day; Mairilek had passed a night disturbed by dreams that broke her sleep as well as his, and from which he woke to make love as if he sought safety in her arms. She wondered if he had contrived to meet the Master, and looked up again, wanting to catch his eye: but he was bending over something at his side. His music box, probably; she smiled. She had been ready that morning to remind him to take it when he went to the Town, but he had needed no prompting, though he had still been strangely low-spirited, seeming more resolved than eager to seek the musicians.

The Old Mistress was among the last to take her seat, coming in only a little ahead of the musicians. As she sat she leaned across to her successor and muttered, "Harinel has kept the Master on a leash all day, the pompous fool. He never did know when to leave alone. I hear the man had to ask outright for time alone to pray and practice." Rahiké met her eyes dismayed, and she shook her head. "The boy won't have had a chance to get near him. Still, there must have been time to talk to the others."

Rahiké's heart ached with disappointment. She acknowledged the musicians' bows composed, but her eyes followed Lodge Master Harinel with indignant anger. Perhaps Mairilek had seen the younger men, but what use was that? How could they help him? It was the Master he needed.

Shadows gathered under the roof, filling the little

booth and hiding Mairilek's face from her. She saw the shape of him leaning forward as the young musicians played; once she thought one of them glanced up at him, and he moved his hand, perhaps in greeting. Herself, she hardly heard them, except for the boy who sang so sweetly. For him to have come so near meeting a Master of his craft, and then to be thwarted by the self-importance of a man who could care nothing for their guest, was infuriating. Lamps were lit after a while. She was able to see Mairilek more clearly, but none of her glances caught his eye; he was never looking at her. Most of the time his gaze was withdrawn; he did not even watch the players. Then the Master Musician came forward.

Mairilek moved, leaning on the front of the box. The lamplight caught him, and people seeing him for the first time stared and whispered, but he did not notice. He heeded nothing but the leather-clad man on the stool. Whenever the music had paused there had been a stir and mutter of conversation, as there was now; the young men had played even when there was not silence, but their Master did not. He did not speak, nor even look about, only set his hands on his knees and waited: and the room grew still. Only then did he pick up his instrument. Rahiké glanced at Mairilek. She saw his eyes flash about the room, over the people all respectful attention for the Master; and his look asserted, *You will do that for me some day!* At other times such innocent arrogance only moved her to tender amusement: now, suddenly, she was frightened.

The music drew her gaze back to the Master, and presently bent it to the floor. The pure remote sound rose like cold smoke, and she drew back from it. Once she looked at Mairilek, and saw his face; she did not look again. The river of music dragged at her, numbing her mind, filling her with panic as she struggled in the element she could not breathe. Beside her she heard the Mistress sigh occasionally, presumably with pleasure. For herself, she cared only to shelter her heart.

Afterwards, Rahiké did not see when her lover left. He still sat unmoving in the booth as the room emptied and the Mistress talked to the musicians; he had not joined the applause, only leaned back on the wall. Then the next time she looked his place was empty. A group had gathered about her, talking, and she roused herself. Little by little the melancholy passed, the music faded; her spirits began to revive. He had heard the Master, at least; and there would be other years.

By the time she reached the porch it was deserted. Night had fallen, warm and purple, faintly moonlit. She and her companions stood talking a little longer; then the other women bade her a good night and walked off. They moved to the stairs at the far end of the porch, those leading to the Market; but Rahiké turned to the stairway that went down into the great court.

The stairs were of stone, and her feet made no sound on them. She had not gone ten steps on the first flight, so the court below was still hidden from her and she from it, when she stopped between one stair and the next. It was Mairilek's voice that arrested her: and the other was just as unmistakable, no man in Naramethé spoke with that ring. So they had met. She was flushed with gladness; very briefly, and then gladness was altogether gone.

Her lover's voice had brought her to a halt, but it was the expression of it that held her motionless, her hand against the wall, and thickened the blood in her veins. She had never heard him speak so. Never, in all their time together, had he sounded so energetic, so alive. There was not a trace of gentleness in his voice now; there was fire, there was urgency. A picture came to her, of an unleashed falcon thrusting up into the sky. The pain of it blurred her eyes, and it was some moments before she could attend to what was being said. When she did she had not listened long before she thought, This is craft-talk, I have no right to hear this. Yet she stayed where she was, silent by the wall.

Mairilek was tipping out all his ideas at the Master's

feet, throwing them about as he searched for the important ones. He was eager, diffident, assertive by turns. He was describing some of the matters he had tried to talk about to her, that she had never understood—but Master Sarak did. It was obvious that ideas were leaping between them. Well, this was what she had hoped for. For this she had asked the musicians to come. Now she stood transfixed by grief. Several times the Master answered questions laid before him; then one made him pause, and ask to hear it again. He said,"I don't know. I never heard of that. Tell me once more." His voice had been interested, now it became surprised and respectful. Their voices tangled for a while, then Mairilek went on, to Rahiké increasingly imcomprehensible. The Master spoke less and less.

Suddenly the Master said, "Let me hear your voice. Sing this note; now this; and this. . . ." After a while she heard him set down the string frame. "A pity it is too late to train it; but we have enough to do, by Karathek! But you can hear. I never met a better ear; perfect. And you have never been taught? Not even the principles?"

"Who was there to teach me? Before tonight I only heard musicians once."

"So everything you know you found for yourself? And you must have made all your music for yourself? Oh, you look confused! Don't you know I played other men's work tonight? Maybe I'll be playing yours before I am old. Come, let me hear some of it. Play to me."

She heard Mairilek fumbling with the cover of his music box, clumsy again, and an exclamation as it slipped from his hands. "What are these?" asked the musician's voice.

Mairilek sounded embarrassed. "Oh—ideas. It is a way I use to hold them until I can work on them."

After a pause Master Sarak said very respectfully, "Karathek be praised, we did not go straight to Karserik: and all the Children of Maha bless your lady! This is a fine instrument; how did you get it?"

There was a silence. Mairilek said in an altered voice, "It came from Halkal-Mari. Master, I—"

"Enough. Don't talk, play. I know what you want to say; that you are ashamed, you cannot play. I will tell you whether you can play. No doubt you need help. But I tell you this, lad," and Rahiké cried out silently, for she called him *tathiki*, as Masters called their apprentices, "I tell you this; I think I have as much to learn from you as to teach you. Now play. Anything; play the first thing you made for yourself."

Mairilek touched the strings hesitantly. "You mean the first real music?" Rahiké clenched her teeth.

"Yes, whatever that means."

He hesitated again, then said, "I can't play you that, it doesn't belong to me. Hear this."

Master . . . Enough to do . . . To teach you . . . Tathiki. Rahiké thought, I should not have listened. This is a mystery. I must go. But she remained there, motionless, feeling the world turn to fire and ice about her.

Dreaming Voiha rose high above the world, and Karathek followed her. By the time Rahiké reached her house, her steps dragged with weariness, and her thoughts had to be moved like her feet, one at a time, with effort. She opened the door of Burdal's room and looked at the child sleeping, the big dog on the floor beside her; Siké was gone, she was late. "Sleep well, baby," she whispered, and closed the door. She stood in the middle of the room, staring out of the window for a long time before she made herself move. What was she waiting for? For him to come bounding up the hillside, burning with excitement, eager to tell her of his talk with the strangers? He would not come. She shivered faintly, and said aloud, "No, not tonight." She went out again to fetch the porch dog, then closed the door and drew the blinds.

The night had grown cool, and seemed colder as she lay down on the bed and drew the quilt up to her breast.

She did not sleep. She lay awake, gazing into the darkness, pondering on what she had done. Yet could she wish it undone? If she could reach back to that moment in Sikas, would she change it? She thought of his voice as he talked to the Master, changed, as if for the first time he had filled his lungs with air. Could she grudge that? But she moaned as she turned toward his side of the bed. Karinané, Flame Kindler, Lady of Fire, you are a cruel Goddess. Patiently you coax us and teach us to trust you, and then—

Rahiké stretched her arm across his place on the mattress, wondering if he would ever lie there again; and it was fear, not security, that answered her.

Morning came like any other morning, except that Rahiké woke to a world grown strange to her. She went out onto the porch in the dawn and stared across at the Town, as if the answer to the question that tortured her might be written above its roofs; but it looked as it always did. So many sunrises had seen her there, watching Mairilek go down the slope. Now the dog came to her and went away whimpering.

There were the same tasks waiting for her as any day—Burdal to care for, the house, the dogs—and she did not want the child to sense anything amiss. There was grief to be feared for her too. So she carried herself calmly, though her soul was trembling, and only once, when she looked at the place where his music box usually stood, did she feel the dizziness threaten her. Burdal and Heffa walked with her most of the way to the City, but when they turned away along the path to the Children's Court a veil of fear fell around her. She could think of nothing but her blindness, her foolhardiness. Was this the foresight of her pride, was this the woman who was thought fit to guide and protect a nation, and she could not see the snake in her own path? Had she walked with head too high, anxious for where others trod, heedless of her own feet?

Substance and safety had gone out of the world. Even the path to the Mistress's House seemed strange. She would have been amazed to know how little her outward demeanor was altered. Though she hardly saw the women she met, she greeted them with unchanged smiles and instinctive replies; only the Old Mistress saw a difference in her. She looked at Rahiké's still eyes and answered her greeting quietly, without asking after Mairilek.

Rahiké began work calmly, but it was very hard to keep her mind on what she did. Elsewhere in the Mistress's House, in the City, she heard only the usual noises, no commotion, no concern, though it seemed to her that the news she waited for should be blazoned across the sky. The morning wore on, and she began to feel sick and weak with tension. Her hands trembled, and several times she answered the Mistress haltingly. The Mistress watched her, troubled, but remained silent until Rahiké, unable to keep longer from the subject that obsessed her, said, "I had thought the Master Musician would have been here before this, if they have to make much of their journey today."

The Mistress fidgeted with her work, then said unwillingly, "He has been, Rahiké. He came very early, before you were here. He saluted you respectfully."

The Young Mistress sat back, shaking. The shock untied her bones. So she had been sitting here waiting for nothing, and maybe even now, maybe while she had been busying herself with meaningless tasks that would all have to be done again anyway—it was nearly noon. They would be gone by now.

Rahiké was on her feet, rolling papers. The weakness had left her. Why was she wasting the day here? "Your pardon, Mistress, I must go," she said. "I thought the man would come here, or I would have been at the Town long before this."

The Mistress nodded, looking at her unhappily, and watched her to the door. "Rahiké!" she said; then, awkwardly,

"Keep your heart up, successor. All may be well in the end."

Rahiké paused, her hand on the doorjamb; sighed, nodded. "Yes, I know," she agreed quietly. "When Voiha wakes."

She left the cloudy numbness behind on the road to the Town. The day grew vivid, fierce with dread and hope; her pulse seemed to beat the air around her, though her steps were swift and firm. As she came near the Town the path turned, and she could see through the gate. Far down the central street a knot of people were standing. Sweat sparkled her skin, a faintness swept over her. Two men stood talking at the gate, but they broke off and stared as she approached. She went on without faltering, remembering the excuse she had chosen, though she knew it would deceive no one. She said, "A fine morning, craftsmen. Where will I find Lodge Master Harinel?"

One of them looked at her in silence, but the other said, "There is no knowing today, Young Mistress." His voice was excited and eager. She asked, "Why, is something amiss in the Town?" He answered, "Master Dairek of the Potters' Lodge has lost his apprentice Mairilek. He has gone north out of the Town to follow the musicians."

She had known it as soon as she saw how they looked at her. Now she kept her dignity and endured their eyes, saying only, "Oh? I thought they were going south." She stepped past them and entered the Town, knowing they turned to look after her, knowing they were not deceived. The thought pierced her that there would be this to endure all over Naramethé; sympathy would be plentifully mixed with spite, and everyone would be watching to see how she bore her loss. She faced them alone now; and the first rush of pure grief filled her.

It was a very long time since she had been in the Town, and she was not sure which was the Potters' Lodge.

However, she judged it likely that the crowd had gathered there, and walked toward it. Hardly a man in the Town was working, it seemed; all the porches and balconies were thronged. They all watched her as she passed, erect under the weight of their stares. But she found it a little easier to gather her strength as she approached the crowd. Shock and anger helped her, for two women stood at the center of it: Mekiné and Tiridal.

Mekiné had an arm about her mother; the older woman was weeping shamelessly, and railing at Master Dairek. Groups of interested, shocked, annoyed men stood about. Dairek, an aging fat man, with hair gray as the clay on his apron, stood stolidly listening to Tiridal. She was crying, "You should have stopped him! He was your apprentice! A fine Master, to let this happen!"

The men noticed Rahiké, and their interest sharpened. Dairek stared at her and answered Tiridal loudly, "I was never the lad's Master! He was never apprenticed to my craft!"

The crowd muttered a little at his words. Rahiké said calmly, "Master Dairek: I regret the loss to your Lodge." Behind her someone laughed, and her face heated as she turned to the women. "Come, Tiridal, Mekiné, you should not be here."

Master Dairek said, "There is no loss to my Lodge, Young Mistress. The lad would never have made a potter!"

Tiridal raised her voice again. "Could you not teach him? Who could I trust to look after him if not you? You should have stopped him!"

"Should I put chains on my doors?"

"Tiridal! Be silent!" Rahiké spoke so sternly that the mother turned from Dairek to her. "Master Dairek is right, he had no duty to keep Mairilek leashed. And you have no right to question him. This is a matter for the Town. The Master is not to blame, and if he were he would not be answerable to you—only to his brothers and to Karathek."

The man cried again, "Should I put chains on my doors?" Rahiké looked at him, seeing for the first time the anguish in his face. His features must always have had too much strength for comeliness, but there was splendor in the dark eyes under his heavy brows. Now they burned with grief; she saw them full of tears as he repeated, "The lad was never apprenticed to my craft!"

At last Rahiké and Mekiné each took an arm of Tiridal and forced her as gently as they could out of the Town. Mekiné had been silent all the while, but her face was quaking, and as soon as they were out of sight of the Lodges her tears burst out. When they stood still Rahiké turned to Tiridal and said, "How could you forget yourself so? To shame the City before the Town!"

"Why should I care?" cried Tiridal. "They let my boy go with the strangers. They didn't stop him!"

"If you love him, be glad of it! If he had stayed he would have been nothing all his life but a laughing-stock. Now he can be about his true craft, he will be a Master. Would you rather he played all his life in your yard? I tell you, he is a great craftsman, they will speak his name in Halkal-Mari before long. Can you grieve for that?"

But even Mekiné sobbed and stared bitterly at her, and Tiridal was not consoled. "Yes, Madam, well may you say it! This is all your doing! It was only you turned his mind from his Lodge, encouraging him with that music. He would never have done this but for you. He would have made a potter, he was a good boy, he would have settled down!"

Rahiké cried, "A good boy? He is a man twenty-four years old! And next spring they would have made him a laborer—not a potter, a laborer! Did you never think of that? *He* knew it! Now he will be what Rehera made him to be. You dare not complain of it. By the Holy Fire you dare not! They will honor him through Halilak; they will make offerings to him some day!"

Tiridal pulled the cloth from her head and covered

her face with it, wailing. Rahiké looked at her friend and
said, "Take her home, Mekiné. Mekiné! Can you not bear
it, if I can?"

But Mekiné drew away from her, her eyes hostile,
and said, 'Don't speak to me: I am his sister!" The hurt of
it made Rahiké step back. "Take her home!" she cried
harshly, and left them.

Her only thought was to get home. Since the night
before she had faced this possibility, believing she knew
the pain it would bring; but she was wrong. Something
impossible had happened, and she struggled in vain to
grasp it. To leave Naramethé— it was like a leaf leaving its
tree; she could not have guessed he would do it. Images
rose in her mind, of the musicians, hard and weatherbeaten;
of the Master, leather-clad and rough-haired, and beside
them of Mairilek combed and fresh, Mairilek vine-crowned
in his scarlet festival kilt, Mairilek in his white wool tunic.
They did not belong together. Would he wear flowers in
his hair again? Would he grow a beard?

She had taken the less direct path that led through
the woods, not knowing why until she was under the
trees; then, safe from observation, she began to run.
There were no tears in her, only agony and terror. Her
heart cried, This cannot happen! But her mind replied, Of
course it can, it has happened to others, why not to you?
Spare me, she begged: Great Rehera, why do you do this
to me? And reason answered, relentless, But if you are
spared, he is sacrificed. There is not enough happiness to
go round.

She paused, gasping, leaning against a tree. She had
not outdistanced grief; it circled her like a panting dog.
She put her hands to her head, wanting to scream, feeling
that if she could scream loudly enough this would all be
driven away, but she knew it was not so. She did raise her
head and cry, "Mairilek!" but to speak his name called the
agony down on her, and she pushed away from the tree
and ran on. Leaving the wood behind she remembered
how he had run so, that first evening, and how she had

stood watching. The dogs began to bark as she neared the house, and she raised her head. The door was open, and Mairilek stood there.

Rahiké stopped; then flung herself forward again. He had not gone. No tears had softened her pain, but they came now, flooding up with the surge of gratitude. The weight of her limbs was turned to a fiery lightness. She should not have doubted him, doubted Rehera. He loved her: she should have trusted him.

He had stepped back into the house. She leapt up the stairs, calling to him, and did not stop running until she caught him in her arms. He grasped her fiercely, hiding his face in her neck in silence. She clung round his shoulders, exulting to feel his body against hers, warm, solid; there: there. "They said in the Town that you had gone!" she cried. "I thought you were gone!" As she spoke she opened her eyes, and her gaze went over his shoulder. She saw the bundles on the floor even as he said, "You thought I would go without seeing you?"

The pain that went through her then left only emptiness behind. She held him tightly still, not wanting him to feel her shock, understand her mistake. There was bitterness enough to come; she must not make the parting harder for him. Only when she thought she had lost her stricken look did she gently loosen her clasp and step back. Then she saw his haggard face; he looked as if the last glow of boyhood had died in him. "Oh, Mairilek!" She touched his cheeks. He grasped her wrists and leaned his brow against hers. He said hoarsely, "I have promised to follow them. They are waiting for me on the road to Karserik. Rahiké, I don't want to go. I shall die. I have sworn to go!"

She raised his head and freed her hands. "Come," she said gently. "Sit down. Tell me everything. Where have you been? In the Town they think you have gone already."

"I went out of the Town with Master Sarak and the others, but I would not leave until I had seen you. They did not press me; they said they would wait. I went north to Ranek's Shrine, and then I came here. I had not thought—I was not thinking—that you would be at the City. That I would have to wait here, with all this"—his eyes went unhappily around the room—"but I would have waited all day. I would not have gone without seeing you."

"I am sorry for thinking it; I was not thinking either. Oh, my love, you look exhausted!"

"I have not slept. Master Sarak was talking to me all night. All night till dawn. At first, when he began, it was wonderful. I asked him so much, I played to him—oh, I was flying, Rahiké. Then he said he wanted me to go with them." He looked at her and tried to smile, and could not. "That broke my wings. I told him at first that I could not. That I could not leave you. But he persuaded me. He used every note he could play. He was kind, he was angry, he argued, he was scornful, he commanded me . . . He said, about you; he said the gods would thank you for what you had done; he praised you, Rahiké, he called you a Queen, said you were wise, you knew, you intended this."

He looked sorrowfully at her, and she shook her head, whispering, "No, I am not so wise. Nor so brave. But how did you see him? I heard Master Harinel would let no one near him."

"No . . . It was the others. I went to the Guest Lodge yesterday morning, and saw them." He paused; for the first time a faint smile warmed his eyes. "You know I had been afraid of them; but it was not like that. They made me welcome. They listened to me. They took me in. I could hardly believe it." His hands gripped each other. "Rahiké, I loved Master Dairek, I have tried to be loyal to the Potters' Lodge—but I felt it, then. The brotherhood. The craft-bond. I never felt it before." She sat still and looked at him, letting the blood run down in silence.

"They said I must talk to the Master, and they would tell him so. And after they left the Assembly House, when Master Harinel tried to keep me away, they almost carried him off. So I saw Master Sarak." His eyes fell, and he was silent for a moment. "Well, I have told you. Rahiké, he tells me I could be a great Master; greater than him. He says I have a gift from Karathek himself, that I am one whose head and hands he kissed. He says—he says—" He swallowed. "He says I have—he thinks I have—he said, 'I will venture a prophecy.'" His voice took on the Master's strange tone. "He said, 'If you serve Karathek as you should, soon there will be Lodges for our craft in every Town in Halilak; you will win this for us.'" He looked at her, wretched. "That is what he said. Rahiké, I must go. When I said last night that I would follow him, he took me straightway to Karathek's temple and made me swear it with my hands on the doorpost. I know why he did it. He thought he must bind me, because when I saw you I would not want to go. And he was right."

She wanted to hold him and cry, Don't leave me, I shall die, don't go; but she could not. It would only tear his heart, embitter his new life; and it would cast a shadow over all his memories of her. Even without his oath, nothing could keep him now. He had found his craft-brothers, his Master, the life he had been born for. She could not hold him now; so since he must go, let him go whole. She made herself say steadily, "Of course you must go. I believe everything he says of you. I knew you had to meet him. Mairilek, you want to go. I know you do."

He muttered, "Yes, I want to go. I knew, yesterday, in the Lodge with the others. But I want to stay, too. I love you, Rahiké! I can't bear it. If they go without me, they take my pride as a craftsman with them: and if I go, I leave you. However I choose, I lose half my life."

She put her arms round him and said shakily, "Then you must go with the greater half. You can bear it. We can bear more than we think, more than we want to. Oh, my love, don't grieve. Go with a whole heart! I don't want to lose you, never think it, but—you must have your craft. I always knew it. Oh, Mairilek! But, you said once, if you were not what you are I might not love you, and it was true, it still is and this only happens because of what you are; so I must love—that is, I must not—"

Her voice died in confusion. He said, "I would have done anything for you; and all I can do in the end is make you unhappy. Forgive me."

She cried with a passion that sounded like anger, "Forgive you? Forgive you for what? For being what you are, when that is what I love? Never say such a word! You shone too bright in my life not to cast a shadow. Maha makes them too. Should I forgive her?"

But she looked at him, and knew also that it was true, she could not live without him. She could breathe, talk, work, but she could not live. Her soul would fall silent, and close its wings: and she could not tell him.

She turned away, seeking for ordinary things to say. "Have you food for the journey? Do you need money? Mairilek, you are going to Halkal-Mari, you will play in the presence of the Queen! Perhaps—we shall meet there—" Then he stood too, and said her name, and she could not be calm any longer.

"Hiramarrek!" she cried through her tears. "When I first saw you, I thought you were Hiramarrek, and I was right; only I am Nehaté after all, and you must flee me, for you would certainly die if you stayed."

"No, it is not true! Everything I have is your gift. Even my Master, my brothers, it is you who gave me them. You have given me my life."

She wept. "Then I have done enough. Don't let me take it away again. If you were to lose by my loving you, then indeed I would have lived for nothing."

She was holding him again. He lifted his hand to her headcloth with the familiar gesture, then hesitated, and let it fall. She raised her face. He kissed her, groaned when he had to let her go, and kissed her again. "Go now, you must go!" she whispered: yet she drove her face into his neck, hiding in his hair, seeking darkness, blindness, a way to avoid the coming moment.

Rahiké never knew how she found the strength to end that embrace, but somehow they were standing apart, and then he was slinging his belongings about him. "Burdal—I can't wait long enough to see her—"

"I will tell her what you would want. It's better like this." She thought suddenly of the other child, that he would never love now; but there was no point in telling him. She walked beside him to the door, feeling nothing at the last but a strange and terrible lightness. On the threshold he stood and looked at her. Haggard, disheveled, how could he be so beautiful? She leaned on the door. To say good-bye and know it was forever, it was impossible. To part never to meet again, it could not be faced; could not be acknowledged. He said desperately, "We will come to Naramethé. I shall see you then. If I may."

She could imagine. A few days, every year, every few years? And all the life of the year sucked into those days. She said, "Yes. You know this door is open whenever you come to it." He muttered, "I said I would wait to be jealous of the lovers who came after me." She kissed his cheek. "And I told you, you will wait a long time."

When he was gone she stood at the window watching him out of sight. The dogs whimpered, running out to him, and he turned aside to caress them. Then he walked away, and he did not look back. She stood there thinking, I did this. His walk now was slow—grief as well as his burdens dragged at him—but Rahiké knew it would not always be so. The road that led from her was also the road that led to his craft-brothers, and to the glory that belonged to him. He would walk lightly again. Already he had the love that would heal him, console him for what he had lost. Maybe he would never love another woman, but he would have what he had always loved most. While she...she knew she was maimed. Burdal, Naramethé, her son, all of them could not make her whole. For her, spring was over, and the time of flowering would not come again.

After he had vanished she remained there, bemused. She imagined him years hence, a Master, wholly in command of his Power. He would grow great in Halkal-Mari.

The Queen among Queens would know his name. All Halilak would know it, and know him for what he did. His beauty had ceased to matter. When he died he would be a hero to whom craftsmen prayed. She would never see his gray hair now.

She stood in silence, gazing into emptiness. She did not weep; it would take many weeks to unlock her tears. Tears were for lesser grief. Burdal would weep, when she knew. She would cry loudly and bitterly, raising her voice against a world that took her beloved from her. But Rahiké knew that tears change nothing; tears have never moved the Gods. Her heart rose, and she pushed it down; learning the lesson Mairilek had learned as a small boy: enduring reality.

I was born in London right at the end of World War II of mixed Irish, Cornish, Somerset, West Highland stock, with the Sun and Moon in Capricorn and Aquarius rising—thus giving Saturn three places on my birth-sign, which is not fair. So I started off with a promising identity crisis and this was improved when, at two, we moved to rural Essex. Perhaps this accounts for the verbal and intellectual precocity which made me, very unwillingly, a rather lonely child.

I have been asked why I write fantasy. First, I am sure I would have written, anyway. And I did not intend to write for public consumption. In early days I thought it purely private and that if I wrote for publication it would be "realistic" novels. . . . I learned to read very early, at two-and-a-half. At five I had an almost adult reading ability, but adult books were more than the child could cope with. So I found the great store of literature that age and popularity have reduced to emotional simplicity—not that "reduced" is the word, but the emotions are clear, basic, strong, while the stories can be told in rich, exciting language—folktale, myth, and legend. These, with the later addition of history, were my diet. Oddly I read very few children's classics: Ransome, a little Nesbit, Treece, Saville. But my knowledge of children's books was professionally gained later when I became a librarian. Nor did I encounter adult fantasy until I was twenty.

So my head was stuffed with heroes, quests, castles, oaths, causes, Kings, Gods; and not surprisingly when I began to write that is what came out.

As for the specific form, Vandarei, it began as a playworld, the sort that a lot of children have, and I was of course the Queen, the character about whom I created the adventures. But I had the disposition of a pedant. I didn't really want to pretend: I wanted to know, to be sure, to get it right. So even in its childish form this playworld had a tendency to become concise, factual. As I grew older, horses became a passion and the playworld developed into "Equitania"—the horse motif strengthening. During this time the history of the country itself assumed an importance and I began to actually write. At fifteen, however, the last links with "Equitania" wavered and the name "Vanderei" appeared. The Queen was abandoned and ceased to be an avatar of myself, becoming a character whom I manipulated, but with whom I no longer especially identified.

*Read this preview of the beautifully written
and illustrated giftbook*

THE
HIGH
KINGS

by Joy Chant
Illustrated by George Sharp

A Bantam Hardcover

THE CELTS—that artistically rich, magnificent people whose legendary history culminated in the heroic reign of King Arthur—have long been a source of wonder for many. Their heritage is a treasure trove: stories of epic heroism, of women who fought alongside their men, of giants and towering challenge, of ultimate sacrifice joyously given, of vaulting courage and high humor, of myth, magic, marvel—and through it all, the scarlet thread of tragic realism that governed a people beset by the constantly recurring threat of extinction.

Because the Celts themselves had no written tradition, Joy Chant has chosen to tell their magnificent legends as they had been told in their own time—by bards around a campfire, or at the courts of their High Kings. And for time and place she has chosen the last great Celtic court—that of King Arthur—setting each tale within a framework that includes a note about the historical or cultural background. Each legend is illuminated by the paintings of George Sharp, who worked closely with the author and editor every step of the way. In addition to the full color plates and the illustrations, David Larkin, art designer for the book, has selected Celtic decorative patterns, maps, and reproductions of their marvelous bronze and gold artifacts to enhance the stories and notes.

The result is high drama, an extraordinary overview of the legends of the Celts, placing them in relation to the state of mind of Arthur's people as they gather themselves for the final defense of their way of life.

While we can only begin to tell you about the magnificent artwork and design that grace this book, you can read a sample of Joy Chant's evocative storytelling from THE HIGH KINGS on the following pages....

Brutus of Troy was the first High King of the Island of the Mighty. Imogen, his Queen, bore him three sons, Locrin and Kamber and Albanac, and the Island did not hold their match. Locrin was without equal for beauty, Kamber for wisdom, and Albanac for boldness. They were all three generous and valiant, and the love between them ran strong and joyful.

In his old age Brutus decided to divide the inheritance among them and he pondered how to do so justly. He called bold Albanac and instructed him to make three divisions of the Island. Albanac made the lands north of Humber one realm; that was the largest, but few men were dwelling there and there were desolate places in the north of it. West of Severn he made another, and there the wisest men of the Island were wont to gather, and the bards. The third realm was the richest; Thames flowed through it, and London was there, and it lay between Humber and Cornwall where Corineus was King.

"Now that is well done," said Brutus. Then he added, jovially, summoning Locrin, "The youngest has divided, let the eldest choose." And that has been the custom of Britain ever since. Locrin chose the mid-part of the Island, Kamber took the West, leaving the North for Albanac; and those realms were ever after called with their names, Logris and Cambria and Albany.

When his years were fulfilled Brutus died, and the Britons mourned him and made him a rich grave. Locrin was High King after him and wore the crown of London. Still he loved most to be with his brothers, and he did not go wooing; until the people though they loved him began to say, "Is the High King a youth or a man? A King without children is but half a King." Then the elders of Britain came to Locrin and said, "Lord, it would be well for you to choose a wife."

The thought did not displease Locrin. Indeed he had been thinking about it himself. He said, "It would be well, but there are many fair and well born maidens in Britain. How should I choose?"

The elders asked, "Is there no lady whom you love?"

Their handsome King grinned, "No, for all alike delight me! Come, advise me. If there is one more worthy than the rest, tell me."

They answered, "Corineus, King of Cornwall, has a daughter. None could be more fitting for the place at your side."

"Is she fair?" Locrin returned.

"Indeed she is!"

"Then I will see the maiden." Thus Locrin agreed to journey into Cornwall.

There, in high summer, he was the guest of great Corineus, and a feast was made for him. The daughter of Corineus came into the feast; she was beautiful and proud, and her name was Vennolandua. The red berry of the rowan was not more glorious than her hair, nor its blossom whiter than her skin. Her brows were black and fine, and the glance of her eyes bright as the glance of a falcon on a cliff. Her dress was of green silk, gold-embroidered, and she wore a gold torc about her neck, with fair gold bracelets red-enamelled on her white arms. The bards when they sang praise to her need sing no more than truth.

She bore mead to Locrin in a cup of fine workmanship, and when she looked on him and saw his beauty which had no like in Britain her heart grew warm. Locrin saw her tall stately figure and her bearing like a queen and he could find no fault with her. It was clear she would make a fit partner for the High King and accordingly he asked that she should be his wife.

In those days it was the custom to perform a thing in the same half of the year in which it was planned, lest ill luck follow; so that those betrothed in summer-half were married before Samhain. Accordingly, a day was appointed on which Locrin and Vennolandua should sleep together, when the trees change to russet and gold, and she would then depart with him to his home. Meanwhile Locrin returned to his own kingdom.

But before the time was come that he should fetch Vennolandua from her father's house a grief befell Britain. A foreign people came to the Island, landing in Albany. Under their chieftain Humber, they began to ravage the land to the North.

In fury, Albanac said to his elders, "This land was given to my father Brutus and to his kinsmen, and to no others. Let us drive those strangers out!"

But the elders of his people argued, "Lord, the men of Albany are few. It would be well to summon your brothers with their warbands."

Albanac roared at them, "And shall I always be sheltering behind my brothers' shields? Before the Gods, I will not do it. I desire this deed and this praise for myself!" For Albanac was the youngest of the three.

Accordingly, he gathered his warriors about him, and they mounted in their chariots and went out against Humber. Then there was trampling and hacking, thrusting of spears and denting of shield-bosses, and the noise of groans and cries. Wherever the fight was thickest Albanac was there, running out on the yoke-pole of his chariot to hurl his spears, shouting and exhorting his warband. Fierce was the onslaught; but by reason of the great numbers of the invaders the men of Albany were overcome, and young Albanac was slain.

When Locrin and Kamber heard of it they came together, and great was their grief. Lamenting him they cried out, "Alas for the hair that was yellow and curling as the flower of the broom, there is dust and blood upon it! Alas for the cheek where no beard had grown, it was red as the foxglove, now it is pale! Alas for our brother, the shining hawk of battle, the handsome merry youth; there is neither speech nor laughter in him now, and the eagle feasts on his flesh!"

Then they resolved to be avenged for Albanac and to drive out the invader. They called their warriors to them, a great host, and their speed into the north was such that the turves cut by the hooves of their horses hung over them so thickly, it would be thought a flock of birds was there.

Word of it came to Corineus and straightaway he called for Vennolandua and said to her, "It is a bad portent, daughter, but it is necessary to name another time when you may become the wife of Locrin even though I fear that time may be beyond Samhain and the year's turning, in winter-half."

But she said only, "It is not fitting to talk of weddings when there is fighting to be done."

Humber brought his army into Logris, and at the border Locrin and Kamber met him and fell upon him. The face of the sun was hidden with the dust that went up from the battle, and the din of it was louder than a fierce storm in winter when the sea contends with the rock. The men of Britain had the victory, and the invaders fled them. Though Humber escaped from the battle, in his flight he fell into the river and was drowned, and many of his people with him; and for that it bears his name. Then the Britons cut off the heads of their enemies and made heaps of them.

The ships of their enemies were near that place, and they seized them and all that was in them, and divided the spoil. Locrin had gold and treasure for his portion, and there were also young women in the ships, captives of the invaders. Among them was a woman of such beauty that when Locrin beheld her it seemed to him there could be none so lovely and perfect among the women of the world. She was as white as the swan, as the snow of a single night, as a lily on a lake. The yellow of her hair was more pale than the petal of the primrose, and her eyes were the sky of spring. Her bearing was all gentleness and grace, and when she stood before Locrin she wept so that her tears like pearls fell through her slim fingers. The heart of Locrin melted in him; he chose her for his own, and that very night he lay with her. She had been the concubine of Humber before; she was a woman of Germany, and her name was Estrildis.

From that time Locrin was continually in the company of the slim shining girl, and his love for her grew until it was past measure. He was not content that she should be his mistress, but he desired to make her the Queen at his side.

When this was known, the men about him were uneasy and displeased. "It is fitting," they said, "that the High King should have a beautiful woman to sleep with him, but this woman is a foreigner and a slave, and she is not worthy to be Queen of the Island of the Mighty."

They went to Kamber to ask him to persuade his brother not to marry her. Kamber the Wise came to Locrin to reason with him. "Though the woman is fair as the first light of morning, yet she is not fit to be your wedded companion," he said. "It would be better for you to marry the daughter of Corineus."

"It is not clear to *me* that it would be better to lose the company of the girl I love so dearly."

"Yet there is a reason," said Kamber.

"Tell it to me."

"You will fulfill your oath in doing so."

"That is a heavy reason," said Locrin, "but not so heavy as would be the parting from Estrildis."

"I have another reason. Your marriage with Vennolandua would bind Cornwall to Logris."

"Cornwall is a rich realm," said Locrin, "but a richer treasure is my lovely gentle girl."

"I have another reason."

Locrin sighed. "Very well, tell it to me," he said.

"It is no better to insult Corineus than to insult a god. Terrible will his anger be if you put this slight on his daughter."

"That is a fierce reason," said Locrin, and he fell silent. Then he said, "To please the people and to avoid strife I will marry Vennolandua. But I will not send Estrildis from me."

His brother embraced him, and relieved that he had won Locrin to his view, Kamber said, "In this you must do as seems good to you. But as for the marriage it is far better for you to decide as you have than for the people to appoint a man to judge you."

"Indeed," exclaimed Locrin, "that would have shamed me."

Then Locrin returned to London, and he called magicians and bade them make a hiding place for Estrildis. They hollowed out a great cave under the city, and the air of it they made sweet, and there were fruit trees and springs of water in it, nor was it dark. In that cavern Locrin hid Estrildis, and she dwelt there.

When all was safe, he went to the house of Corineus with the bride-gifts and the maiden-fee for Vennolandua, and he fetched her to his own house. She had heard word of Estrildis, and when she came to London she kept jealous watch. But she found no trace of her rival, nor any rumor, for none knew of the secret cavern, but all thought that Locrin had sent the girl from him. Then Vennolandua was content, and believing that the heart of Locrin had returned to her, loved him as much for his imagined faithfulness as she already did for his great beauty. But Locrin continually went in secret to the cavern under London.

In time Vennolandua bore a son and they called him Maddan. When he was grown to boyhood he was sent to be fostered with Corineus.

Estrildis also bore a child, a fair daughter, and her name was Savren. In all the years that passed Locrin never ceased to visit his mistress, and his love for her was undiminished.

There came a time when age was heavy on great Corineus, and he died. All the Britons mourned him, the slayer of Gogmagog, the champion of Britain, and they buried him richly. Great was the grief of Vennolandua for her father, and Locrin mourned without feigning; nevertheless a fear was gone from him. The longing to make Estrildis his Queen was still in him, and now the dread of that mighty man no longer restrained him.

Accordingly, when the funeral of Corineus was past and the mourning over, he summoned the chief men of the kingdom and told them that he proposed to put Vennolandua away and make another his wife. And this time he would not listen to counsel.

When this word came to the Queen she bade her

women bring her mirror, saying, "Has my cheek grown hollow, or my eye dull?"

"Lady, it is not so," they answered her, looking to see her weep. But a terrible anger filled her. She rose up, and she robed and adorned herself, and went to Locrin.

When she stood before him she said, "What is this that you will do? When you asked me of my father Corineus it was not said this was to be a temporary marriage. Were there no bride-gifts at our wedding? Did I not leave my father's house to dwell in yours?" Her great eyes flashed as she spoke and she flung her words like spears. "Have I brought you no alliance? Are the men of Cornwall without mettle, or their chariots few? Do the warriors I maintain, feasting them on meat and wine, not carry their spears at your command? Have I contrived against you, or betrayed your honour?"

The High King looked at her, and saw her tall and majestic, with an eagle's glance; and he thought of Estrildis of the soft speech, and was silent.

Then the Queen stamped her foot upon the ground and demanded, "Answer me, *husband*! I am the lady of most renown in Britain, and so I was when you married me. Will you now set me aside for one who is a slave?"

For a space, Locrin did not speak, but fingered the carving of his chair. At last he raised his eyes and said heavily, "Lady, I choose to do so." And that was all the answer he made her.

Then fire came into her eye, she shook out her burning hair and the blaze of her anger burst from her. "Is it in your mind that because Corineus is dead the blood of Cornwall is grown tame?" she cried. "By mountain and by sea, *you will find it is not so!*"

With that, she whirled and strode from the room, her garments fluttering in the wind of her raging departure. Immediately she gave orders to gather all that was hers together, and working deep into the night she put all her affairs in order. Then summoning the warriors she maintained, with their chariots and charioteers, and leaving nothing that was hers in London, she set out straightaway and returned to her own realm.

Locrin said to himself, "Maddan is young, and he is my son also, and there is no other man of her house." And he had no fear of her anger. Then he fetched Estrildis from her hiding place and set her by his side, making her wife and Queen of Britain, and his daughter Savren also he raised to honour. So there was great joy among the three of them that they were all together in the sight of men and the light of day.

When Vennolandua came to Cornwall and to her own house, her kinswomen came out to meet her, lamenting the shame that had been put upon her. But she was the daughter of Corineus, and her mettle was not less than his.

"This is no time for weeping," she said. She sent for her son Maddan, and embraced him. He was a goodly boy, though far from manhood, and Corineus had trained him well in arms. Vennolandua told him, "My curse is upon Locrin, that he should put this slight upon one of the blood of Brutus and Corineus, upon a gold-torqued Prince of Britain!"

But her son answered her stoutly, "The shame that is put on me is bad, but worse by far is the shame on you and on my fosterfather Corineus. If he lived you would not lack a champion." Then he hesitated, looking up at her. "But now I am troubled for it is ill for a son to fight against his father."

She embraced him again and quietly she said, "I shall not ask it of you, my son."

Then she went about Cornwall and ordered the craftsmen to make weapons and chariots. All Cornwall filled with the clangour of the forges and their fires burned by day and by night. From the horsefields she chose horses for the chariots, and the four finest she chose for herself.

She summoned the master of all the smiths and bade him make weapons for her, helmet and shield, long spears and short spears and the barbed spear and sword. Fit for the Lady of Battles he made them;

Govannon himself could have wrought no better. They were inlaid with gold and white bronze and fine enamelling; the short spears flew to their target as if they had sight, and the long spears had each a ball of gold on the butt of them.

Then Vennolandua called a muster of the men of Cornwall, and they gathered to the royal dun. There she made a feast for them, setting fresh pork before them and filling their cups with mead; for a year meat and drink did not fail them, nor the singing of bards.

At the end of a year she armed herself and appeared before them, and called upon them to avenge the insult to her and to the house of Corineus. They rose with a great shout and took up their weapons. Nor did they scorn to follow a woman to battle, for she was the daughter of Corineus and the battle-rage was upon her so that she appeared like one of the goddesses who delight in battle and in offerings of slain men. Until that time it had not been customary with the women of Britain to go to war, but it was the custom after.

She mounted into her chariot, and her son Maddan was standing by. He spoke formally to the Queen, "I wish success to your venture, swiftness to your wheels, sharpness to your weapons, and the protection of seven shields about you!" But then, moving closer, he murmured, "Oh, my mother, it is hard to take leave of you. I wish I did not have to stay here!"

"Not so," smiled Vennolandua, "for it is time that you were a shield-bearer." At that he mounted joyfully beside her. Then the men of Cornwall went forth, and their warrior Queen led them.

They entered Logris, and began to ravage the land. Wherever they went they burned and despoiled, driving off cattle and leaving ruin in their wake. The bards that were with them continually sang praises to Vennolandua while mocking and satirising Locrin so that his name had no honour in the land.

Men came to the High King to tell him of it. "Lord, make haste and go forth against the Queen of Cornwall, for she is laying waste the land and your people are in fear of her; also the bards make satires upon you."

"Alas," Locrin grieved, "how can I do this thing? How can you ask this of me? The woman has lain at my side and her son is my son."

"Nevertheless, Lord," they insisted, "if you do not, the country will be utterly destroyed." And at last Locrin called his warband about him and summoned his chief men to bring their warbands. Then he went forth against the army of Cornwall.

Locrin sent out men on swift horses to find where the army of the Queen might be, and they found her and came into her presence. They said to her, "What is the cause that you bring armed men into Logris and make war upon the King of Britain?"

Vennolandua answered harshly, "Tell that crooked-tongued oath-breaker who brings dishonour to the name of Brutus that I come seeking a bull of mine that has gone astray!"

They returned to the High King with all speed. "It is not hard to find the Queen," they reported, "for where she is there is smoke rising."

Between the Stour and the Severn the two hosts met. The spears of the men of Cornwall were thick as barley, and the sound of the hooves and of the wheels of their chariots upon the earth was like the roar of the landslide when a hill falls into the valley. Not less was the army of Logris, and the day grew dark with the dust of battle.

In the midst of the field Vennolandua and Locrin met together. Locrin cried out, "Lady, you do wrong to bring spears against me, for the Coronet of Cornwall is subject to the Crown of London!"

"Do you bleat to *me* of wrongs?" she raged. "What of the wrong done to me and to my son?" Then she shook her spears and challenged in a great voice so that all might know of it: "Hear me!" Her call went out over the host. "I am Queen of the Island of the Mighty, and bitter to me is the sight of my people dying, since the quarrel is between the High King and myself only. Let none fight but only he and I."

Locrin's heart was sick and heavy. He said only, "It is better so."

Then the carynx was blown and the two hosts drew apart. The Queen and the High King dismounted from their chariots, and when Locrin saw that Maddan was his mother's shield-bearer tears burst from his eyes. He said to Vennolandua. "Let me embrace my son before we fight."

"You must ask him for that," she said.

"He had better not ask me," said Maddan. "The back of my hand would be my answer!" Then he turned his face from his parents and wept.

Now a dread stillness fell on the hosts and there were no cries of challenge, or insult, or encouragement. In the dusty space between the two watching hosts the King and Queen fought in bitter silence. Locrin was valiant and a man of prowess, but the battle-fury was on Vennolandua so that her frenzy overcame him and he was overthrown, and she slew him.

When the spirit was out of him she cut off his head and held it up before her face and lamented, "Alas for the head that had no equal for beauty, and for the lips that I have kissed! My mouth knew no kisses but yours, my husband, and I remember the weight of your breast on mine. My grief is that your death should come by me; if it were not for the wrong you did me it would not have been so. Mine is the mouth that last shall touch yours," and she kissed him once full on his blood-dabbled lips. That was all the keening she made for him.

Then Vennolandua took the head and tied it by the hair to the timbers of her chariot. Maddan wept to look upon the face of his father, but he said to his mother, "The blow was well struck. Now we are avenged for the shame put upon us."

"Not so," Vennolandua replied, "for there is more." She commanded that Estrildis be brought before her.

When Estrildis came and Vennolandua looked for the

first time upon that gold and white beauty, a great anger filled her. "Before the Gods," she cried, "was it for such a weak, pale thing that Locrin cast me aside? My curse on him, the insult was worse than I knew!" She glared at Estrildis. "Woman, do you see the head of him that was my husband?" But Estrildis hid her eyes, weeping bitterly, for she had indeed seen the head of Locrin, her beloved. "Weep on," said Vennolandua, "water is fitting for you; by water you came to us, by water you shall go."

Then she sent for Savren, and the girl was brought before her. She was a maiden even lovelier than her mother. She was more fair than stars over the sea, or than the star of morning: and all the host fell silent as they looked on her, for she seemed not like a mortal girl but like one from the Earthly Paradise.

Seeing her youth and her innocence, there was not a man there but would have had mercy on her. But Vennolandua saw in the unearthly beauty of the girl an aching echo of the man she had honoured and loved so deeply; and she remembered the wrong done to her son. She commanded that mother and daughter should both be drowned in the great river that was near at hand. Then Estrildis fell down before her and begged for mercy for her daughter. "Spare the child," she entreated, making the only plea she knew might sway the Queen, "for she is of the blood of Brutus. She is your son's sister!"

"She is my son's supplanter," said Vennolandua. She regarded the woman a long moment. "I will not spare her, but for her birth she shall have this honour, that the river shall be called with her name." Then she commanded her warriors to cast woman and girl into the river and it was done.

So Estrildis died, glad of it because of the death of her love. But the people of the Living Land beneath the water had pity on Savren; they took her with them to that happy place where there is no guilt and the young men never grow old, so that she did not perish but lived like one of them. She became the guardian of the river; and still she dwells in bliss under the glassy waters of Severn that bears her name.

Then Vennolandua sat in the chair of Locrin, and ruled as High Queen until her son was a man, when she returned to Cornwall. There have been other Queens ruling over the Island of the Mighty, illustrious women: but the first woman to be exalted with the Crown of London was Vennolandua the warrior Queen.

OUT OF THIS WORLD!

That's the only way to describe Bantam's great series of science fiction classics. These space-age thrillers are filled with terror, fancy and adventure and written by America's most renowned writers of science fiction. Welcome to outer space and have a good trip!

FANTASY AND SCIENCE FICTION FAVORITES

Bantam brings you the recognized classics as well as the current favorites in fantasy and science fiction. Here you will find the most recent titles by the most respected authors in the genre.

☐	23365	THE SHUTTLE PEOPLE George Bishop	$2.95
☐	22939	THE UNICORN CREED Elizabeth Scarborough	$3.50
☐	23120	THE MACHINERIES OF JOY Ray Bradbury	$2.75
☐	22666	THE GREY MANE OF MORNING Joy Chant	$3.50
☐	23494	MASKS OF TIME Robert Silverberg	$2.95
☐	23057	THE BOOK OF SKULLS Robert Silverberg	$2.95
☐	23063	LORD VALENTINE'S CASTLE Robert Silverberg	$3.50
☐	20870	JEM Frederik Pohl	$2.95
☐	23460	DRAGONSONG Anne McCaffrey	$2.95
☐	20592	TIME STORM Gordon R. Dickson	$2.95
☐	23036	BEASTS John Crowley	$2.95
☐	23666	EARTHCHILD Sharon Webb	$2.95

Prices and availability subject to change without notice.

Buy them at your local bookstore or use this handy coupon for ordering:

Bantam Books, Inc., Dept. SF2, 414 East Golf Road, Des Plaines, Ill. 60016

Please send me the books I have checked above. I am enclosing $_____ (please add $1.25 to cover postage and handling). Send check or money order —no cash or C.O.D.'s please.

Mr/Mrs/Miss _____

Address_____

City_____ State/Zip_____

SF2—11/83

Please allow four to six weeks for delivery. This offer expires 5/84.